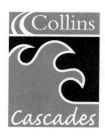

War Stories:
A Cascades collection of fiction and non-fiction

ED. CHRISTOPHER MARTIN

Cascades consultants:
John Mannion, former Head of English, London
Sheena Davies, Principal Teacher, Glasgow
Adrian Jackson, General English Advisor, West Sussex
Geoff Fox, Lecturer at the University of Exeter School of
    Education, and a National Curriculum Advisor
Emily Rought-Brooks, Head of English, London

Collins
Cascades

Other titles in the **Collins** *Cascades series that you might enjoy:*

Miles Ahead: A *Cascades* book of travel writing
ED. WENDY COOLING

This selection of the most entertaining and inspiring travel writing has been edited by Wendy Cooling, widely known in schools for her work as a literary consultant.

ISBN 000 711 259 9

As it Happens: A *Cascades* book of reportage
ED. ROSY BORDER

Fascinating and occasionally unbelievable first-hand accounts of great events, terrible situations and epic discoveries, selected by an experienced author and former journalist.

ISBN 000 711 364 1

Wild World: A *Cascades* book of non-fiction
ED. ANNE GATTI

The natural world and the amazing field of scientific discovery have led to some powerful and influential writing over the years. This accessible and stimulating collection ranges from Darwin to Attenborough.

ISBN 000 711 166 5

For further information call 0870 0100442
fax 0141 306 3750
e-mail: Education@harpercollins.co.uk
website: www.CollinsEducation.com

ED. CHRISTOPHER MARTIN

War Stories:

A *Cascades* collection of fiction and non-fiction

War, the Red Angel, the Awakener
The Shaker of Souls and Thrones; and at her heel
Trail grief, and ruin, and shame!

W.E. Henley: 'Epilogue'

To Peter Robins

Published by HarperCollins*Publishers*,
77–85 Fulham Palace Rd, London W6 8JB

Selection and activities copyright © Christopher Martin

ISBN 000 711 485 0

First published in Great Britain by HarperCollins*Publishers* 2001
Reprinted 2002
The right of Christopher Martin to be identified as the author of this work is
asserted.

British Library Cataloguing in Publication Data
A catalogue record for this book is available from the British Library.

Cover design by Ken Vail Graphic Design, Cambridge
Cover illustration: Laying Telephone Wire, c.1919 by Colin Unwin Gill
(1892–1940) – supplied by the Bridgeman Art Library. We have been unable
to trace the copyright holder of Laying Telephone Wire and would be
grateful to receive any information as to their identity.
Manufactured in China
Commissioned by Thomas Allain-Chapman
Edited by Gaynor Spry
Production by Katie Morris

Contents

Preface

War has two faces. It can seem exciting, spectacular, full of episodes of extraordinary courage and sacrifice. Or it can simply appear to be a horrific catalogue of cruelty, killing and destruction. In a 1905 poem, 'The Shrine of the War God', B. Paul Neuman visualised war as a splendid, eye-catching building, which draws you towards it. Once you enter, you see the true horror.

> Splendid, upon a bare and blasted plain,
>   It rose before me in the sunset light,
> Vast, many towered, like some majestic fane[1]
>   With one great cross of gold to crown its height.
>
> And then I looked within; a poison breath
>   Sickened me, and I saw the temple's Lord
> Stalk up and down his festering house of death,
>   A naked savage with a dripping sword –

This collection of stories, some famous, some little-known, some fiction, some non-fiction, reflects this two-sided vision of human conflict. The authors took part in or imagined the great wars of the nineteenth and twentieth centuries. They record the bravery and comradeship but also the futility, waste and death.

Modern battles are too vast for an individual to understand: he or she can only see a tiny corner of the action. The short story form is therefore a good way of dealing with war experience: it sets a scene quickly and boldly; it portrays a character or two; it builds up to a point of revelation or

---

[1] *fane*: temple

excitement; sometimes it reflects on a theme. The non-fiction pieces record reality more closely: the writers observe events with precise, sensory detail so that we can share the war experience that they describe.

On reading these stories, we relive moments of history. We become the man waiting to be hanged on the Civil War bridge; the gas-masked young officer leading his men into a sea of mud; the nurse horrified at the contents of the latest ambulance train; a 'Hurricane' pilot chasing German bombers over London; the infantryman gingerly testing the ground for mines in Vietnam. These stories make war memorials and museums come alive. They also complement the work of the brilliant war poets – that young readers know so well – in showing what Wilfred Owen called:

'The pity of war, the pity war distilled.'

Crimean War (1854–1856)

Russian claims to parts of the Ottoman (Turkish) Empire were disputed by Britain, France, Austria and Turkey. An Allied force landed near Balaclava on the Russian Crimean peninsula in the Black Sea. For eleven months, they besieged the nearby Russian naval base of Sebastopol. Half a million men died in the notoriously badly managed war, many from disease.

The Charge of the Light Brigade: 25 October 1854

The three reports that follow describe the Charge of the Light Brigade, one of the most famous, and futile, events in military history. Its background needs some explanation.

Russian ambitions to expand southwards into the crumbling Turkish Empire forced France and Britain to declare war in March, 1854. An Allied army of 60,000 men gathered in Turkey and then landed in the Crimea, in southern Russia, to besiege the Russian naval base at Sebastopol. In October, a Russian force of 30,000 men counterattacked, hoping to cut off the Allied siege forces from their supply base at Balaclava.

North of Balaclava lay two wide valleys, Northern and Southern, divided by a ridge, the Causeway Heights, on which defensive forts had been built. Early on October 25, the Russian cavalry captured these forts and swept on into the Southern valley, threatening Balaclava. An extended line of Highland infantry, the 'thin red streak', stood firm against the Russian charge, until the British Heavy Brigade of cavalry drove it back. The Russians retreated over the Heights, taking away the fort guns as they did so.

Lord Raglan, the British Commander, saw all this from a hill near Balaclava, where his staff officers stood, 'as though they were looking on a stage from the boxes of a theatre'.

To lose guns meant battle defeat. The Light Brigade, an elite cavalry strike force, commanded by Lord Cardigan, had been waiting in the Northern valley. Raglan sent a vague order, carried by a Captain Nolan, to Lord Lucan, overall commander of the British cavalry. The Light Brigade should 'advance rapidly and prevent the enemy from carrying off the guns'. Lucan could not see the fort guns but knew there was a thirty-gun Russian battery a mile and a half away at the end of the Northern valley. Yet the order was unclear. 'Attack, sir. Attack what?' he asked Nolan who, despising Lucan, pointed vaguely at the end of the valley and answered insolently, 'There, my lord, is the enemy. There are the guns.'

Lucan passed the order to Cardigan. Both men knew that there were Russian guns on each side of the valley, and more guns and cavalry waiting at its end. But neither could disobey an order. Cardigan shouted, 'The Brigade will advance' and the trumpeter sounded the gallop. As the men, in splendid uniforms with swords drawn, rode forwards, Nolan tried to redirect them to the Heights but was killed by the first Russian shell.

In twenty minutes it was all over. 673 men began; 113 were killed and 134 wounded. Some escaped shells and bullets only to be cut down by Russian cavalry on the way back. Hundreds of horses were

killed or wounded, making the Light Brigade ineffective for the rest of
the war. A French general who watched the whole episode commented,
'It is magnificent, but it is not war. It is madness ... '.

Resources for pages 9–31

Books *The Crimean War* by Paul Kerr
Videos *The Charge of the Light Brigade* and *Balaclava*, both by Cromwell
    Productions
Websites www.pinetreesweb.com/13th-balaclava.htm

Watching the Charge

William Howard Russell from *The Times* (14 November 1854)

W.H. Russell (1820–1907) was an Irishman who became the most famous reporter who ever worked for The Times. *He was the only war correspondent in the Crimea. His brilliant reports, sent home to be published three weeks after events, allowed readers to see and hear the war:*

'The silence is oppressive – between the cannon bursts one can hear the champing of bits and the clash of sabres below'.

The Times, *under a great editor, John Delane, dominated the British press: its circulation was five times greater than all the other papers put together. Delane's powerful editorials supported Russell's reports: he praised 'the progress of the cavalry through and through that valley of death' concluding that 'the British soldier will do his duty ... even to certain death, and is not paralysed by feeling that he is the victim of some hideous blunder'.*

And now occurred the melancholy catastrophe which fills us all with sorrow. It appears that the Quartermaster General, Brigadier Airey, thinking that the Light Cavalry had not gone far enough in front when the enemy's horse[1] had fled, gave an order in writing to Captain Nolan, 15th Hussars, to take to Lord Lucan, directing His Lordship 'to advance' his cavalry nearer to the enemy ...

I should premise[2] that, as the Russian cavalry retired, their infantry fell back towards the head of the valley, leaving men in three of the redoubts[3] they had taken and abandoning the fourth. They had also placed some guns on the heights over their position, on the left of the gorge. Their cavalry joined the reserves, and drew up in six solid

---

[1] **horse:** cavalry (soldiers on horseback)

[2] **premise:** say first

[3] **redoubts:** forts

divisions, in an oblique line, across the entrance to the gorge. Six battalions of infantry[4] were placed behind them, and about thirty guns were drawn up along their line, while masses of infantry were also collected on the hills behind the redoubts on our right. Our cavalry had moved up to the ridge across the valley, on our left, as the ground was broken in front, and had halted in the order I have already mentioned.

When Lord Lucan received the order from Captain Nolan and had read it, he asked, we are told, 'Where are we to advance to?'

Captain Nolan pointed with his finger to the line of the Russians, and said, 'There are the enemy, and there are the guns, sir, before them. It is your duty to take them,' or words to that effect, according to the statements made since his death.

Lord Lucan with reluctance gave the order to Lord Cardigan to advance upon the guns, conceiving that his orders compelled him to do so. The noble Earl, though he did not shrink, also saw the fearful odds against him. Don Quixote[5] in his tilt against the windmill was not near so rash and reckless as the gallant fellows who prepared without a thought to rush on almost certain death ...

As they passed towards the front, the Russians opened on them from the guns in the redoubts on the right, with volleys of musketry and rifles.

They swept proudly past, glittering in the morning sun in all the pride and splendour of war. We could hardly believe the evidence of our senses! Surely that handful of men were not going to charge an army in position? Alas! It was but too true – their desperate valour[6] knew no bounds, and far indeed was it removed from its so-called better part – discretion. They advanced in two lines, quickening their pace as they closed towards the enemy. A more fearful spectacle was

---

[4] **infantry:** foot soldiers
[5] **Don Quixote:** an elderly knight. In Cervantes's famous story, Don Quixote, the knight, thought windmills were giants that he should fight.
[6] **valour:** courage

never witnessed than by those who, without the power to aid, beheld their heroic countrymen rushing to the arms of death. At the distance of 1200 yards the whole line of the enemy belched forth, from thirty iron mouths, a flood of smoke and flame, through which hissed the deadly balls. Their flight was marked by instant gaps in our ranks, by dead men and horses, by steeds[7] flying wounded or riderless across the plain. The first line was broken – it was joined by the second, they never halted or checked their speed an instant. With diminished ranks, thinned by those thirty guns, which the Russians had laid with the most deadly accuracy, with a halo[8] of flashing steel above their heads, and with a cheer which was many a noble fellow's death cry, they flew into the smoke of the batteries; but ere[9] they were lost from view, the plain was strewed with their bodies and with the carcasses of horses. They were exposed to an oblique[10] fire from the batteries on the hills on both sides, as well as to a direct fire of musketry.[11]

Through the clouds of smoke we could see their sabres flashing as they rode up to the guns and dashed between them, cutting down the gunners as they stood. The blaze of their steel, as an officer standing near me said, was 'like the turn of a shoal of mackerel'. We saw them riding through the guns, as I have said; to our delight we saw them returning, after breaking through a column of Russian infantry, and scattering them like chaff, when the flank fire of the battery on the hill swept them down, scattered and broken as they were. Wounded men and dismounted troopers flying towards us told the sad tale – demigods[12] could not have done what they had failed to do. At the very moment when they were about to retreat, an enormous mass of lancers was hurled upon their flank. Colonel Shewell, of

---

[7] **steeds:** horses
[8] **halo:** circle of light
[9] **ere:** before
[10] **oblique:** diagonal
[11] **direct fire of musketry:** rifle fire
[12] **demigods:** half men/half gods

the 8th Hussars, saw the danger, and rode his few men straight at them, cutting his way through with fearful loss. The other regiments turned and engaged in a desperate encounter. With courage too great almost for credence,[13] they were breaking their way through the columns which enveloped them, when there took place an act of atrocity without parallel in the modern warfare of civilised nations. The Russian gunners, when the storm of cavalry passed, returned to their guns. They saw their own cavalry mingled with the troopers who had just ridden over them, and to the eternal disgrace of the Russian name the miscreants[14] poured a murderous volley of grape and canister[15] on the mass of struggling men and horses, mingling friend and foe in one common ruin. It was as much as our Heavy Cavalry Brigade could do to cover the retreat of the miserable remnants of that band of heroes as they returned to the place they had so lately quitted in all the pride of life.

At twenty-five to twelve not a British soldier, except the dead and dying, was left in front of these bloody Muscovite[16] guns.

---

[13] **credence:** belief
[14] **miscreants:** evildoers
[15] **grape and canister:** shot fired from guns
[16] **Muscovite:** from Moscow in Russia

Activities

Close study (newspaper reportage: non-fiction recount text)
1 Russell sets the scene by picturing the battlefield. What does he tell us about it in the opening paragraphs?
2 What impressions do we get of the main characters before the Charge?
3 In describing the Charge, Russell uses some striking comparisons, both similes (direct) and metaphors (indirect). Which is most memorable?
4 Russell shows distaste for the Russian enemy. Which words and phrases express this?

Language study
5 Russell uses the techniques of the skilled journalist:
  • quotations from eye-witness participants
  • observation of what he saw, and heard, of the Charge
  • colloquial style (questions, exclamations, broken sentences) to engage the reader.
  Find examples of all of these in the passage.
6 Russell shows the Charge as glorious but futile. Find some words and phrases which express the glory and glamour of the Charge. Find other words that show it as an ugly, pointless waste of brave young lives.

Writing
7 Many Victorian poets were inspired to write about the Charge after reading Russell's report. Alexander Smith described:
  'The trampling thunder and the blaze of steel –
  The terror and the splendour of the charge ... '
  Alfred Tennyson wrote:
  'When can their glory fade?
  O the wild charge they made!
  All the world wondered.'
  Read the whole of Tennyson's famous poem and discuss which words and ideas he took from Russell (and Delane).
8 Then write your own poem about the Charge with two contrasting verses:
  • one about the Light Brigade before and during the attack
  • one about the survivors, and the dead, after the Charge.
9 See page 30 for a question on comparison of all three passages on the Crimean War.

Reading
10 *Theirs But to Do and Die* by Patrick Waddington contains all the Victorian poems written about the Charge.

A Lancer's Experience

James Wightman from *The Nineteenth Century Magazine* (May 1892)

James Wightman, of the 17th Lancers, took part in, and survived, the Charge. Having reached the Russian guns, his horse was shot from under him on the return, and he was wounded and then captured. In May, 1892, he vividly recalled his experiences in The Nineteenth Century Magazine.

As we stood halted here, Captain Nolan, of the 15th Hussars, whom we knew as an aide-de-camp[1] of the head-quarter staff, suddenly galloped out to the front through the interval between us and the 13th, and called out to Captain Morris, who was directly in my front, 'Where is Lord Lucan?' 'There,' replied Morris, pointing – 'there, on the right front!' Then he added, 'What is it to be, Nolan? – are we going to charge?' Nolan was off already in Lord Lucan's direction, but as he galloped away he shouted to Morris over his shoulder, 'You will see! You will see!'

I cannot call to mind seeing Lord Lucan come to the front of the Light Brigade and speak with Lord Cardigan, although of course I know now that he did so. But I distinctly remember that Nolan returned to the brigade, and his having a mere momentary talk with Cardigan, at the close of which he drew his sword with a flourish, as if greatly excited. The blood came into his face – I seem to see him now; and then he fell back a little way into Cardigan's left rear, somewhat in front of and to the right of Captain Morris, who had taken post in front of his own left squadron. And I remember as if it were but yesterday Cardigan's figure and attitude, as he faced the brigade and in his strong hoarse voice gave the momentous word of command, 'The brigade will advance! First

---

[1] **aide-de-camp:** officer assisting senior officer

squadron of 17th Lancers direct!' Calm as on parade – calmer indeed by far than his wont on parade – stately, square and erect, master of himself, his brigade, and his noble charger, Cardigan looked the ideal cavalry leader, with his stern firm face and his quiet soldierly bearing. His long military seat was perfection on the thoroughbred chestnut[2] 'Ronald' with the 'white stockings' on the near hind and fore, which my father, his old riding-master, had broken[3] for him. He was in the full uniform of his old corps, the 11th Hussars, and he wore the pelisse,[4] not slung, but put on like a patrol jacket, its front one blaze of gold lace. His drawn sword was in his hand at the slope, and never saw I man fitter to wield the weapon.

As I have said, he gave the word of command, and then turning his head toward his trumpeter, Britten of the Lancers, he quietly said, 'Sound the Advance!' and wheeled his horse, facing the dark mass at the farther end of the valley which we knew to be the enemy. The trumpeter sounded the 'Walk'; after a few horse-lengths came the 'Trot'. I did not hear the 'Gallop', but it was sounded. Neither voice nor trumpet, so far as I know, ordered the 'Charge'; Britten was a dead man in a few strides after he had sounded the 'Gallop'. We had ridden barely two hundred yards and were still at the trot, when poor Nolan's fate came to him. I did not see him cross Cardigan's front, but I did see the shell explode, of which a fragment struck him. From his raised sword-hand dropped the sword, but the arm remained erect. Kinglake[5] writes that 'what had once been Nolan' maintained the strong military seat until the 'erect form dropped out of the saddle'; but this was not so. The sword-arm indeed remained upraised and rigid, but all the other limbs so curled in on the contorted trunk as by a spasm, that we wondered how for the moment the huddled form kept the saddle. It

---

[2] **chestnut:** brown horse

[3] **broken:** trained

[4] **pelisse:** fur-lined cloak of Hussar

[5] **Kinglake:** another Charge survivor

was the sudden convulsive twitch of the bridle hand inward on the chest that caused the charger to wheel rearward so abruptly. The weird shriek and the awful face as rider and horse disappeared haunt me now to this day, the first horror of that ride of horrors.

As the line at the trumpet sound broke from the trot into the gallop, Lord Cardigan, almost directly behind whom I rode, turned his head leftward toward Captain Morris and shouted hoarsely, 'Steady, steady, Captain Morris!' The injunction[6] was no doubt pointed specially at the latter, because he, commanding the regiment one of the squadrons of which had been named to direct, was held in a manner responsible to the brigade commander for both the pace and direction of the whole line. Later, when we were in the midst of our torture, and, mad to be out of it and have our revenge, were forcing the pace, I heard again, high above the turmoil and din, Cardigan's sonorous[7] command, 'Steady, steady, the 17th Lancers!' and observed him check with voice and outstretched sword Captain White, my squadron leader, as he shot forward abreast of the stern disciplined chief leading the brigade. But, resolute man though he was, the time had come when neither the commands nor the example of Cardigan availed to restrain the pace of his brigade; and when to maintain his position in advance, indeed, if he were to escape being ridden down, he had to let his charger out from the gallop to the charge. For hell had opened upon us from front and either flank, and it kept open upon us during the minutes – they seemed hours – which passed while we traversed[8] the mile and a quarter at the end of which was the enemy. The broken and fast-thinning ranks raised rugged peals of wild fierce cheering that only swelled the louder as the shot and shell from the battery tore gaps through us, and the enfilading musketry fire[9] from the Infantry in

---

[6] *injunction:* order
[7] *sonorous:* loud
[8] *traversed:* crossed
[9] *enfilading musketry fire:* rifle fire from the side

both flanks brought down horses and men. Yet in this stress it was fine to see how strong was the bond of discipline and obedience. 'Close in! close in!' was the constant command of the squadron and troop officers as the casualties made gaps in the ragged line, but the order was scarcely needed, for of their own instance and, as it seemed, mechanically, men and horses alike sought to regain the touch.

We had not broke into the charging pace when poor old John Lee, my right-hand man on the flank of the regiment, was all but smashed by a shell; he gave my arm a twitch, as with a strange smile on his worn old face he quietly said, 'Domino!![10] Chum,' and fell out of the saddle. His old grey mare kept alongside of me for some distance, treading on and tearing out her entrails[11] as she galloped, till at length she dropped with a strange shriek. I have mentioned that my comrade, Peter Marsh, was my left-hand man; next beyond him was Private Dudley. The explosion of a shell had swept down four or five men on Dudley's left, and I heard him ask Marsh if he had noticed 'what a hole that b— shell had made' on his left front. 'Hold your foul-mouthed tongue,' answered Peter, 'swearing like a black-guard, when you may be knocked into eternity next minute!' Just then I got a musket-bullet through my right knee, and another in the shin, and my horse had three bullet wounds in the neck. Man and horse were bleeding so fast that Marsh begged me to fall out; but I would not, pointing out that in a few minutes we must be into them, and so I sent my spurs well home, and faced it out with my comrades. It was about this time that Sergeant Talbot had his head clean carried off by a round shot, yet for about thirty yards further the headless body kept the saddle, the lance at the charge firmly gripped under the right arm. My narrative may seem barren of inci-dents of the charge, but amid the crash of shells and the whistle of bullets, the cheers and the dying cries of comrades, the sense of personal danger, the pain of wounds, and the consuming passion to reach an enemy, he

[10] **Domino:** the game's over
[11] **entrails:** intestines

must be an exceptional man who is cool enough and curious enough to be looking serenely about him for what painters call 'local colour'. I had a good deal of 'local colour' myself, but it was running down the leg of my overalls from my wounded knee.

Well, we were nearly out of it at last, and close on those cursed guns. Cardigan was still straight in front of me, steady as a church, but now his sword was in the air; he turned in his saddle for an instant, and shouted his final command, 'Steady! steady! Close in!' Immediately afterwards there crashed into us a regular volley from the Russian cannon. I saw Captain White go down and Cardigan disappear into the smoke. A moment more and I was within it myself. A shell burst right over my head with a hellish crash that all but stunned me. Immediately after I felt my horse under me take a tremendous leap into the air. What he jumped I never saw or knew; the smoke was so thick I could not see my arm's length around me. Through the dense veil I heard noises of fighting and slaughter, but saw no obstacle, no adversary,[12] no gun or gunner, and, in short, was through and beyond the Russian battery before I knew for certain that I had reached it.

I then found that none of my comrades were close to me; there was no longer any semblance of[13] a line. No man of the Lancers was on my right, a group was a little way on my left. Lord Cardigan must have increased his distance during or after passing through the battery, for I now saw him some way ahead, alone in the midst of a knot of Cossacks. At this moment Lieutenant Maxse, his Lordship's aide-de-camp, came back out of the tussle,[14] and crossed my front as I was riding forward. I saw that he was badly wounded; and he called to me, 'For God's sake, Lancer, don't ride over me! See where Lord Cardigan is,' pointing to him, 'rally on him!' I was hurrying on to support the brigade commander, when a Cossack came at

---

[12] **adversary:** enemy

[13] **any semblance of:** anything like

[14] **tussle:** fight

me and sent his lance[15] into my right thigh. I went for him, but he bolted; I overtook him, drove my lance into his back and unhorsed him just in front of two Russian guns which were in possession of Sergeant-Majors Lincoln and Smith, of the 13th Light Dragoons, and other men of the Brigade. When pursuing the Cossack I noticed Colonel Mayow deal very cleverly with a big Russian cavalry officer. He tipped off his shako[16] with the point of his sword, and then laid his head right open with the old cut seven. The chase of my Cossack had diverted me from rallying on Lord Cardigan; he was now nowhere to be seen, nor did I ever again set eyes on the chief who had led us down the valley so grandly. The handful with the guns, to which I momentarily attached myself, were presently outnumbered and overpowered, the two sergeant-majors being taken prisoners, having been dismounted. I then rode towards Private Samuel Parkes, of the 4th Light Dragoons, who, supporting with one arm the wounded Trumpet-Major (Crawford) of his regiment, was with the other cutting and slashing at the enemies surrounding them. I struck in to aid the gallant fellow, who was not overpowered until his sword was shot away, when he and the trumpet-major were taken prisoners, and it was with difficulty I was able to cut my way out. Presently there joined me two other men, Mustard, of my own corps, and Fletcher, of the 4th Light Dragoons. We were now through and on the further side of a considerable body of the Russian cavalry, and so near the bottom of the valley that we could well discern[17] the Tchernaya river. But we were all three wearied and weakened by loss of blood; our horses wounded in many places; there were enemies all about us, and we thought it was about time to be getting back. I remember reading in the regimental library of an officer who said to his commander 'We have done enough for honour.' That was our humble opinion too, and we turned our horses' heads.

---

[15] *lance:* spear
[16] *shako:* military hat
[17] *discern:* make out

Activities

Close study (memoir: non-fiction recount text)

I   Russell observed the Charge from a distance. Wightman was *in* it: he heard
the vital orders given and saw the horrors of the battlefield at close quarters.
- What impressions are given of Nolan and Lord Cardigan? (Quote details
from the text.)
- What was Nolan's terrible fate?
- Where does Wightman show us the discipline of the Light Brigade?
- What sad and terrible details of deaths of comrades does he recall?
- What does he mean by 'We have done enough for honour'?
- Where does he show admiration for comrades?

Language study

2   Look at some of the quoted speech that Wightman remembers from the
Charge. This adds considerably to the drama of his memories. Write down
some examples from the text. What does each tell you about the soldiers
and their courage in battle?

Writing

3   Imagine you are a Russian gunner who watched the Charge at close
quarters. You write a letter home to your friend in Moscow. Using detail
from the passage, say what you saw and heard before and during the battle.

4   See page 30 for a question on comparison of all three passages on the
Crimean War.

Reading

5   For a classic account of the Charge of the Light Brigade you might like to
read *The Reason Why* by Cecil Woodham-Smith. *The Charge* by Mark
Adkin provides a retrospective reassessment (1996).

An Old War Horse

Anna Sewell from *Black Beauty* (1877)

Anna Sewell (1820–1878) was born into a Quaker family in Norfolk. An ankle injury in youth made her totally dependent on horses for her own mobility. Her only book, Black Beauty *(1877), grew from this dependence and was a protest against the cruel treatment of horses in Victorian times. It was published just before her death in 1878, so that she knew nothing of its enormous success as a classic of young people's fiction.*

Anna Sewell probably learned from Russell about the horrifying fate of horses involved in the Charge: 362 were killed and many others so badly injured that they were shot.

Quaker detestation of war and violence, very unpopular during the war fever of 1854, had a particular force in Black Beauty. *Old Captain, the horse, a Balaclava survivor, ends his story with a bleak comment on the futility of war.*

[To make her points about cruelty, Anna Sewell allows her horses to talk and think like humans. Captain befriends Black Beauty when they are both working as hansom-cab horses in London.]

Captain had been broken in and trained for an army horse; his first owner was an officer of cavalry[1] going out to the Crimean War. He said he quite enjoyed the training with all the other horses, trotting together, to the right hand or to the left, halting at the word of command, or dashing forward at full speed at the sound of the trumpet, or signal of the officer. He was, when young, a dark, dappled iron grey, and considered very handsome. His master, a young high-spirited gentleman, was very fond of him, and treated him from the first with the greatest care and kindness. He told me he thought the life of an army horse was very pleasant; but when it came

---

[1] *cavalry:* soldiers on horseback

to being sent abroad, over the sea in a great ship, he almost changed his mind.

'That part of it,' he said, 'was dreadful! Of course we could not walk off the land into the ship; so they were obliged to put strong straps under our bodies, and then we were lifted off our legs in spite of our struggles, and were swung through the air over the water, to the deck of the great vessel. There we were placed in small close stalls, and never for a long time saw the sky, or were able to stretch our legs. The ship sometimes rolled about in high winds, and we were knocked about, and felt bad enough. However, at last it came to an end, and we were hauled up, and swung over again to the land; we were very glad, and snorted, and neighed for joy, when we once more felt firm ground under our feet.

'We soon found that the country we had come to was very different to our own, and that we had many hardships to endure besides the fighting; but many of the men were so fond of their horses, that they did everything they could to make them comfortable, in spite of snow, wet, and all things out of order.'

'But what about the fighting?' said I; 'was not that worse than anything else?'

'Well,' said he, 'I hardly know; we always liked to hear the trumpet sound, and to be called out, and were impatient to start off, though sometimes we had to stand for hours, waiting for the word of command; and when the word was given, we used to spring forward as gaily and eagerly as if there were no cannon balls, bayonets, or bullets. I believe so long as we felt our rider firm in the saddle, and his hand steady on the bridle, not one of us gave way to fear, not even when the terrible bombshells whirled through the air and burst into a thousand pieces.

'I, with my noble master, went into many actions together without a wound; and though I saw horses shot down with bullets, pierced through with lances, and gashed with fearful sabre² cuts; though we left

---

² **sabre:** sword with curved blade

them dead on the field, or dying in agony of their wounds, I don't think I feared for myself. My master's cheery voice, as he encouraged his men, made me feel as if he and I could not be killed. I had such perfect trust in him that whilst he was guiding me, I was ready to charge up to the very cannon's mouth. I saw many brave men cut down, many fall mortally wounded from their saddles. I had heard the cries and groans of the dying, I had cantered over ground slippery with blood, and frequently had to turn aside to avoid trampling on wounded man or horse, but, until one dreadful day, I had never felt terror; that day I shall never forget.'

Here old Captain paused for a while and drew a long breath; I waited, and he went on.

'It was one autumn morning, and as usual, an hour before daybreak our cavalry had turned out, ready caparisoned[3] for the day's work, whether it might be fighting or waiting. The men stood by their horses waiting, ready for orders. As the light increased, there seemed to be some excitement among the officers; and before the day was well begun, we heard the firing of the enemy's guns.

'Then one of the officers rode up and gave the word for the men to mount, and in a second, every man was in his saddle, and every horse stood expecting the touch of the rein, or the pressure of his rider's heels, all animated, all eager; but still we had been trained so well, that, except by the champing of our bits,[4] and the restive tossing of our heads from time to time, it could not be said that we stirred.

'My dear master and I were at the head of the line, and as all sat motionless and watchful, he took a little stray lock of my mane which had turned over on the wrong side, laid it over on the right, and smoothed it down with his hand; then patting my neck, he said, "We shall have a day of it to-day, Bayard, my beauty; but we'll do our duty as we have done." He stroked my neck that morning, more, I think, than he

---

[3] **caparisoned:** covered with a decorative covering over the saddle
[4] **bits:** mouthpieces (of a horse's bridle)

had ever done before; quietly on and on, as if he were thinking of something else. I loved to feel his hand on my neck, and arched my crest proudly, and happily; but I stood very still, for I knew all his moods, and when he liked me to be quiet, and when gay.

'I cannot tell all that happened on that day, but I will tell of the last charge that we made together: it was across a valley right in front of the enemy's cannon. By this time we were well used to the roar of heavy guns, the rattle of musket[5] fire, and the flying of shot near us; but never had I been under such a fire as we rode through on that day. From the right, from the left, and from the front, shot and shell poured in upon us. Many a brave man went down, many a horse fell, flinging his rider to the earth; many a horse without a rider ran wildly out of the ranks: then terrified at being alone with no hand to guide him, came pressing in amongst his old companions, to gallop with them to the charge.

'Fearful as it was, no one stopped, no one turned back. Every moment the ranks were thinned, but as our comrades fell, we closed in to keep them together; and instead of being shaken or staggered in our pace, our gallop became faster and faster as we neared the cannon, all clouded in white smoke, while the red fire flashed through it.

'My master, my dear master, was cheering on his comrades with his right arm raised on high, when one of the balls, whizzing close to my head, struck him. I felt him stagger with the shock, though he uttered no cry; I tried to check my speed, but the sword dropped from his right hand, the rein fell loose from the left, and sinking backward from the saddle he fell to the earth; the other riders swept past us, and by the force of their charge I was driven from the spot where he fell.

'I wanted to keep my place by his side, and not leave him under that rush of horses' feet, but it was in vain; and now without a master or a friend, I was alone on that great slaughter ground; then fear took hold

---

[5] **musket:** single-shot rifle

27

on me, and I trembled as I had never trembled before; and I too, as I had seen other horses do, tried to join in the ranks and gallop with them; but I was beaten off by the swords of the soldiers. Just then, a soldier whose horse had been killed under him, caught at my bridle and mounted me; and with this new master I was again going forward: but our gallant company was cruelly overpowered, and those who remained alive after the fierce fight for the guns, came galloping back over the same ground. Some of the horses had been so badly wounded that they could scarcely move from the loss of blood; other noble creatures were trying on three legs to drag themselves along, and others were struggling to rise on their fore feet, when their hind legs had been shattered by shot. Their groans were piteous to hear, and the beseeching look in their eyes as those who escaped passed by, and left them to their fate, I shall never forget. After the battle the wounded men were brought in, and the dead were buried.'

'And what about the wounded horses?' I said, 'were they left to die?'

'No, the army farriers[6] went over the field with their pistols, and shot all that were ruined; some that had only slight wounds were brought back and attended to, but the greater part of the noble willing creatures that went out that morning, never came back! In our stables there was only about one in four that returned.

'I never saw my dear master again. I believe he fell dead from the saddle. I never loved any other master so well. I went into many other engagements, but was only once wounded, and then not seriously; and when the war was over, I came back again to England, as sound and strong as when I went out.'

I said, 'I have heard people talk about war as if it was a very fine thing.'

'Ah!' said he, 'I should think they never saw it. No doubt it is very fine when there is no enemy, when it is just exercise and parade, and

---

[6] **farriers:** blacksmiths

sham-fight.[7] Yes, it is very fine then; but when thousands of good brave men and horses are killed, or crippled for life, it has a very different look.'

'Do you know what they fought about?' said I.

'No,' he said, 'that is more than a horse can understand, but the enemy must have been awfully wicked people, if it was right to go all that way over the sea on purpose to kill them.'

---

[7] ***sham-fight:*** pretend battle

Activities

Close study (novel extract: fiction narrative text)

1 What was good and bad about Captain's army experience before the Crimean War began?

2 To Anna Sewell, horses are 'noble willing creatures'. Which horrible details of the Charge show that men have betrayed the animals' trust?

3 What comments about the glamour and futility of war does old Captain make at the end of the extract?

Language study

4 The relationship between Captain and his master is important in this story. Find words, phrases and sentences which show their close bond.

Writing

5 Like Anna Sewell, Thomas Hardy felt great sympathy for animals and hated the cruelty inflicted on them by humans. At Southampton in 1899, he watched horses being shipped to the Boer War in South Africa, and pitied their fate.

Horses Aboard

Horses in horsecloths stand in a row
On board the huge ship that at last lets go:
Whither are they sailing? They do not know,
Nor what for, nor how. –
    They are horses of war,
And are going to where there is fighting afar;
But they gaze through their eye-holes unwitting they are,
And that in some wilderness, gaunt and ghast,
Their bones will bleach ere a year has passed,
And the item be as 'war-waste' classed, –
And when the band booms, and the folk say 'Good-bye!'
And the shore slides astern, they appear wrenched awry
From the scheme Nature planned for them, – wondering why.

Read the poem carefully. Compare it to old Captain's story. What does each say about horses and war? Compare the language used by poet and novelist. Which is more impressive and memorable?

7 (Extracts on pages 9–29) Compare the passages. Consider the subject matter, the point of view of the narrator, the language and the technique.

Which do you think makes the most effective word picture of the Charge of the Light Brigade?

Reading

8 Michael Morpurgo's *War Horse*, about a cavalry horse's experiences in the First World War, is available as a Collins Cascade.

American Civil War (1861–1865)

The Northern Federal[1] government of the USA fought eleven Confederate states of the South. The main issue was slavery, which the North wished to abolish. Hard fighting in many fierce battles, together with disease, caused 600,000 deaths. The Northern victory at Gettysburg, 1863, was decisive in defeating the South. The Union of the north and south of what is now the USA was saved and four million slaves freed.

Resources for pages 32–69

Books *The American Civil War* by B.H. Reid
Videos *The American Civil War* by Cromwell Productions
   The American Civil War by DD Video
Websites //sunsite.utk.edu/civil-war/warweb.html
   www.spartacus.schoolnet.co.uk/USAcivilwarC.htm

---

[1] **Northern Federal:** Northern side

An Occurrence at Owl Creek Bridge

Ambrose Bierce from Tales of *Soldiers and Civilians* (1892)

Ambrose Bierce (1842–1914?), raised on a rough farm in Ohio, had some soldier's training at the Kentucky Military Institute. At eighteen, he enlisted as a drummer boy when the Civil War began in 1861. Thereafter he fought in some of the most murderous battles such as Shiloh (1862) or Chickamauga (1863). He showed courage and skill, and was steadily promoted to the rank of lieutenant.

After the war, he trained himself as a writer, working in England and San Francisco, where he won the nickname of 'Bitter Bierce' for his sardonic, aggressive journalism. Then he turned to short fiction. His impressive Civil War stories were collected as Tales of Soldiers and Civilians *in 1892.*

In later years, separated from his wife, with one son dead in a gun duel and another ruined by alcohol, Bierce toured the old battlefields of his youth.

> *How they come back to me those years of youth when I was soldiering! Again I hear the far warble of blown bugles. Again I see the tall, blue smoke of camp-fires ascending ... and my blood stirs at the ringing rifle-shot of the solitary sentinel.*
>
> From What I Saw of Shiloh

He looked for another war in which to die. 'I'd hate to die between two sheets, and, God willing, I won't,' he told a friend. He decided to join the army of Pancho Villa, who was fighting to overthrow the dictator of Mexico. 'Good-bye,' he wrote in a farewell letter. 'If you hear of my being stood up against a Mexican stone wall and shot to rags, please know that I think it a pretty good way to depart this life. It beats old age, or falling down the cellar stairs.' No-one knows exactly how he died: he disappeared in Mexico in 1914.

'An Occurrence at Owl Creek Bridge' is based on a real military hanging Bierce saw at Shiloh. He shows us a man's thoughts in the seconds before his death. He moves Owl Creek from its real place in Tennessee to Alabama, to make Farquhar's 'escape' more likely.

I

A man stood upon a railroad bridge in northern Alabama, looking down into the swift water twenty feet below. The man's hands were behind his back, the wrists bound with a cord. A rope closely encircled his neck. It was attached to a stout cross-timber above his head and the slack fell to the level of his knees. Some loose boards laid upon the sleepers supporting the metals of the railway supplied a footing for him and his executioners – two private soldiers of the Federal army, directed by a sergeant who in civil life may have been a deputy sheriff. At a short remove upon the same temporary platform was an officer in the uniform of his rank, armed. He was a captain. A sentinel at each end of the bridge stood with his rifle in the position known as 'support', that is to say, vertical in front of the left shoulder, the hammer resting upon the forearm thrown straight across the chest – a formal and unnatural position, enforcing an erect carriage of the body. It did not appear to be the duty of these two men to know what was occurring at the centre of the bridge; they merely blockaded the two ends of the foot planking that traversed it.

Beyond one of the sentinels nobody was in sight; the railroad ran straight away into a forest for a hundred yards, then, curving, was lost to view. Doubtless there was an outpost farther along. The other bank of the stream was open ground – a gentle acclivity topped with a stockade of vertical tree trunks, loop-holed for rifles, with a single embrasure through which protruded the muzzle of a brass cannon commanding the bridge. Midway of the slope between bridge and fort were the spectators – a single company of infantry in line, at 'parade rest', the butts of the rifles on the ground, the barrels inclining slightly backward against the right shoulder, the hands crossed upon the stock. A lieutenant stood at the right of the line, the point of his sword upon the ground, his left hand resting upon his right. Excepting the group of four at the centre of the bridge, not a man moved. The company faced the bridge, staring stonily, motionless. The sentinels, facing the banks of the stream, might have been statues to adorn the bridge. The captain stood with folded arms, silent, observing the work of his subordinates, but making no sign. Death is a dignitary who when he comes announced is to be received with formal manifestations of respect, even by those most familiar with him. In the code of military etiquette[2] silence and fixity are forms of deference.[3]

The man who was engaged in being hanged was apparently about thirty-five years of age. He was a civilian, if one might judge from his habit, which was that of a planter. His features were good – a straight nose, firm mouth, broad forehead, from which his long, dark hair was combed straight back, falling behind his ears to the collar of his well-fitting frock-coat. He wore a moustache and pointed beard, but no whiskers; his eyes were large and dark grey, and had a kindly expression which one would hardly have expected in one whose neck was in the hemp. Evidently this was no vulgar assassin. The liberal military code makes provision for hanging many kinds of persons, and gentlemen are not excluded.

The preparations being complete, the two private soldiers stepped aside and each drew away the plank upon which he had been standing. The sergeant turned to the captain, saluted and placed himself immediately behind that officer, who in turn moved apart one pace. These movements left the condemned man and the sergeant standing on the two ends of the same plank, which spanned three of the cross-ties of the bridge. The

---

[2] **etiquette:** conventions of behaviour

[3] **deference:** respectful conduct

end upon which the civilian stood almost, but not quite, reached a fourth. This plank had been held in place by the weight of the captain; it was now held by that of the sergeant. At a signal from the former the latter would step aside, the plank would tilt and the condemned man go down between two ties. The arrangement commended itself to his judgment as simple and effective. His face had not been covered nor his eyes bandaged. He looked a moment at his 'unsteadfast footing', then let his gaze wander to the swirling water of the stream racing madly beneath his feet. A piece of dancing driftwood caught his attention and his eyes followed it down the current. How slowly it appeared to move! What a sluggish stream!

He closed his eyes in order to fix his last thoughts upon his wife and children. The water, touched to gold by the early sun, the brooding mists under the banks at some distance down the stream, the fort, the soldiers, the piece of drift – all had distracted him. And now he became conscious of a new disturbance. Striking through the thought of his dear ones was a sound which he could neither ignore nor understand, a sharp, distinct, metallic percussion like the stroke of a blacksmith's hammer upon the anvil; it had the same ringing quality. He wondered what it was, and whether immeasurably distant or near by – it seemed both. Its recurrence was regular, but as slow as the tolling of a death knell. He awaited each stroke with impatience and – he knew not why – apprehension. The intervals of silence grew progressively longer; the delays became maddening. With their greater infrequency the sounds increased in strength and sharpness. They hurt his ear like the thrust of a knife; he feared he would shriek. What he heard was the ticking of his watch.

He unclosed his eyes and saw again the water below him. 'If I could free my hands,' he thought, 'I might throw off the noose and spring into the stream. By diving I could evade[4] the bullets and, swimming vigorously, reach the bank, take to the woods and get away home. My

---

[4] *evade:* escape

home, thank God, is as yet outside their lines; my wife and little ones are still beyond the invader's farthest advance.'

As these thoughts, which have here to be set down in words, were flashed into the doomed man's brain rather than evolved from it the captain nodded to the sergeant. The sergeant stepped aside.

II

Peyton Farquhar was a well-to-do planter, of an old and highly respected Alabama family. Being a slave owner and like other slave owners a politician he was naturally an original secessionist[5] and ardently devoted to the Southern cause. Circumstances of an imperious nature, which it is unnecessary to relate here, had prevented him from taking service with the gallant army that had fought the disastrous campaigns ending with the fall of Corinth,[6] and he chafed under the inglorious restraint, longing for the release of his energies, the larger life of the soldier, the opportunity for distinction. That opportunity, he felt, would come, as it comes to all in war time. Meanwhile he did what he could. No service was too humble for him to perform in aid of the South, no adventure too perilous for him to undertake if consistent with the character of a civilian who was at heart a soldier, and who in good faith and without too much qualification assented to at least a part of the frankly villainous dictum that all is fair in love and war.

One evening while Farquhar and his wife were sitting on a rustic bench near the entrance to his grounds, a grey-clad soldier[7] rode up to the gate and asked for a drink of water. Mrs Farquhar was only too happy to serve him with her own white hands. While she was fetching the water her husband approached the dusty horseman and inquired eagerly for news from the front.

---

[5] **secessionist:** supporter of the Southern side
[6] **Corinth:** the Southern base
[7] **grey-clad soldier:** (appears to be) a Southern soldier who wore a grey uniform

'The Yanks[8] are repairing the railroads,' said the man, 'and are getting ready for another advance. They have reached the Owl Creek bridge, put it in order and built a stockade on the north bank. The commandant has issued an order, which is posted everywhere, declaring that any civilian caught interfering with the railroad, its bridges, tunnels or trains will be summarily hanged.[9] I saw the order.'

'How far is it to the Owl Creek bridge?' Farquhar asked.

'About thirty miles.'

'Is there no force on this side of the creek?'

'Only a picket post half a mile out, on the railroad, and a single sentinel at this end of the bridge.'

'Suppose a man – a civilian and student of hanging – should elude the picket post and perhaps get the better of the sentinel,' said Farquhar, smiling, 'what could he accomplish?'

The soldier reflected. 'I was there a month ago,' he replied. 'I observed that the flood of last winter had lodged a great quantity of driftwood against the wooden pier at this end of the bridge. It is now dry and would burn like tow.'

The lady had now brought the water, which the soldier drank. He thanked her ceremoniously, bowed to her husband and rode away. An hour later, after nightfall, he re-passed the plantation, going northward in the direction from which he had come. He was a Federal scout.

III

As Peyton Farquhar fell straight downward through the bridge he lost consciousness and was as one already dead. From this state he was awakened – ages later, it seemed to him – by the pain of a sharp pressure upon his throat, followed by a sense of suffocation. Keen, poignant[10]

---

[8] **Yanks:** Northerners
[9] **summarily hanged:** hanged without a trial
[10] **poignant:** painfully sharp

agonies seemed to shoot from his neck downward through every fibre of his body and limbs. These pains appeared to flash along well-defined lines of ramification and to beat with an inconceivably rapid periodicity. They seemed like streams of pulsating fire heating him to an intolerable temperature. As to his head, he was conscious of nothing but a feeling of fullness – of congestion. These sensations were unaccompanied by thought. The intellectual part of his nature was already effaced; he had power only to feel, and feeling was torment. He was conscious of motion. Encompassed in a luminous cloud, of which he was now merely the fiery heart, without material substance, he swung through unthinkable arcs of oscillation, like a vast pendulum. Then all at once, with terrible suddenness, the light about him shot upward with the noise of a loud plash; a frightful roaring was in his ears, and all was cold and dark. The power of thought was restored; he knew that the rope had broken and he had fallen into the stream. There was no additional strangulation; the noose about his neck was already suffocating him and kept the water from his lungs. To die of hanging at the bottom of a river! – the idea seemed to him ludicrous. He opened his eyes in the darkness and saw above him a gleam of light, but how distant, how inaccessible! He was still sinking, for the light became fainter and fainter until it was a mere glimmer. Then it began to grow and brighten, and he knew that he was rising toward the surface – knew it with reluctance, for he was now very comfortable. 'To be hanged and drowned,' he thought, 'that is not so bad; but I do not wish to be shot. No; I will not be shot; that is not fair.'

He was not conscious of an effort, but a sharp pain in his wrist apprised him that he was trying to free his hands. He gave the struggle his attention, as an idler might observe the feat of a juggler, without interest in the outcome. What a splendid effort! – what magnificent, what superhuman strength! Ah, that was a fine endeavour! Bravo! The cord fell away; his arms parted and floated upward, the hands dimly seen on each side in the growing light. He watched them with a new interest as first one and then the other pounced upon the noose at his neck. They tore it away and thrust it fiercely aside, its undulations[11] resembling those of a water-snake. 'Put it back, put I back!' He thought he shouted these words to his hands, for the undoing of the noose had been succeeded by the direst pang that he had yet experienced. His neck ached horribly; his brain was on fire; his heart, which had been fluttering faintly, gave a great leap, trying to force itself out at his mouth. His whole body was racked and wrenched with an insupportable anguish! But his disobedient hands gave no heed to the command. They beat the water vigorously with quick, downward strokes, forcing him to the surface. He felt his head emerge; his eyes were blinded by the sunlight; his chest expanded convulsively, and with a supreme and crowning agony his lungs engulfed a great draught of air, which instantly he expelled in a shriek!

He was now in full possession of his physical senses. They were, indeed, preternaturally keen and alert. Something in the awful disturbance of his organic system had so exalted and refined them that they made record of things never before perceived. He felt the ripples upon his face and heard their separate sounds as they struck. He looked at the forest on the bank of the stream, saw the individual trees, the leaves and the veining of each leaf – saw the very insects upon them: the locusts, the brilliant-bodied flies, the grey spiders stretching their webs from twig to twig. He noted the prismatic colours in all the dewdrops upon a million blades of grass. The humming of the gnats that danced above the eddies of the stream, the beating of the dragon-flies' wings, the strokes of the water-spiders' legs, like oars which had lifted their boat – all these made audible music. A fish slid along beneath his eyes and he heard the rush of its body parting the water.

He had come to the surface facing down the stream; in a moment the

---

[11] **undulations:** wavy motions

visible world seemed to wheel slowly round, himself the pivotal point, and he saw the bridge, the fort, the soldiers upon the bridge, the captain, the sergeant, the two privates, his executioners. They were in silhouette against the blue sky. They shouted and gesticulated, pointing at him. The captain had drawn his pistol, but did not fire; the others were unarmed. Their movements were grotesque and horrible, their forms gigantic.

Suddenly he heard a sharp report and something struck the water smartly within a few inches of his head, spattering his face with spray. He heard a second report, and saw one of the sentinels with his rifle at his shoulder, a light cloud of blue smoke rising from the muzzle. The man in the water saw the eye of the man on the bridge gazing into his own through the sights of the rifle. He observed that it was a grey eye and remembered having read that grey eyes were keenest, and that all famous marksmen had them. Nevertheless, this one had missed.

A counter-swirl had caught Farquhar and turned him half round; he was again looking into the forest on the bank opposite the fort. The sound of a clear, high voice in a monotonous singsong now rang out behind him and came across the water with a distinctness that pierced and subdued all other sounds, even the beating of the ripples in his ears. Although no soldier, he had frequented camps enough to know the dread significance of that deliberate, drawling, aspirated chant; the lieutenant on shore was taking a part in the morning's work. How coldly and pitilessly – with what an even, calm intonation, presaging, and enforcing tranquillity in the men – with what accurately measured intervals fell those cruel words:

'Attention, company! ... Shoulder arms! ... Ready! ... Aim! ... Fire!'

Farquhar dived – dived as deeply as he could. The water roared in his ears like the voice of Niagara, yet he heard the dull thunder of the volley and, rising again toward the surface, met shining bits of metal, singularly flattened, oscillating[12] slowly downward. Some of them touched him on

---

[12] ***oscillating:*** swinging to and fro

the face and hands, then fell away, continuing their descent. One lodged between his collar and neck; it was uncomfortably warm and he snatched it out.

As he rose to the surface, gasping for breath, he saw that he had been a long time under water; he was perceptibly farther down stream – nearer to safety. The soldiers had almost finished reloading; the metal ramrods flashed all at once in the sunshine as they were drawn from the barrels, turned in the air, and thrust into their sockets. The two sentinels fired again, independently and ineffectually.

The hunted man saw all this over his shoulder; he was now swimming vigorously with the current. His brain was as energetic as his arms and legs; he thought with the rapidity of lightning.

'The officer,' he reasoned, 'will not make that martinet's[13] error a second time. It is as easy to dodge a volley as a single shot. He has probably already given the command to fire at will. God help me, I cannot dodge them all!'

An appalling plash within two yards of him was followed by a loud, rushing sound, *diminuendo*,[14] which seemed to travel back through the air to the fort and died in an explosion which stirred the very river to its deeps! A rising sheet of water curved over him, fell down upon him, blinded him, strangled him! The cannon had taken a hand in the game. As he shook his head free from the commotion of the smitten water he heard the deflected shot humming through the air ahead, and in an instant it was cracking and smashing the branches in the forest beyond.

'They will not do that again,' he thought; 'the next time they will use a charge of grape.[15] I must keep my eye upon the gun; the smoke will apprise me – the report[16] arrives too late; it lags behind the missile. That is a good gun.'

---

[13] **martinet:** disciplinarian
[14] **diminuendo:** decreasing in volume
[15] **grape:** shell that scatters shot
[16] **report:** explosion

Suddenly he felt himself whirled round and round – spinning like a top. The water, the banks, the forests, the now distant bridge, fort and men – all were commingled and blurred. Objects were represented by their colours only; circular horizontal streaks of colour – that was all he saw. He had been caught in a vortex and was being whirled on with a velocity of advance and gyration that made him giddy and sick. In a few moments he was flung upon the gravel at the foot of the left bank of the stream – the southern bank – and behind a projecting point which concealed him from his enemies. The sudden arrest of his motion, the abrasion of one of his hands on the gravel, restored him, and he wept with delight. He dug his fingers into the sand, threw it over himself in handfuls and audibly blessed it. It looked like diamonds, rubies, emeralds; he could think of nothing beautiful which it did not resemble. The trees upon the bank were giant garden plants; he noted a definite order in their arrangement, inhaled the fragrance of their blooms. A strange, roseate light shone through the spaces among their trunks and the wind made in their branches the music of aeolian harps.[17] He had no wish to perfect his escape – was content to remain in that enchanting spot until retaken.

A whizz and rattle of grapeshot among the branches high above his head roused him from his dream. The baffled cannoneer had fired him a random farewell. He sprang to his feet, rushed up the sloping bank, and plunged into the forest.

▶ All that day he travelled, laying his course by the rounding sun. The forest seemed interminable;[18] nowhere did he discover a break in it, not even a woodman's road. He had not known that he lived in so wild a region. There was something uncanny in the revelation.

By nightfall he was fatigued, footsore, famishing. The thought of his

---

[17] *aeolian harps:* stringed boxes that sound in the wind
[18] *interminable:* endless

wife and children urged him on. At last he found a road which led him in what he knew to be the right direction. It was as wide and straight as a city street, yet it seemed untravelled. No fields bordered it, no dwelling anywhere. Not so much as the barking of a dog suggested human habitation. The black bodies of the trees formed a straight wall on both sides, terminating on the horizon in a point, like a diagram in a lesson in perspective. Overhead, as he looked up through this rift in the wood, shone great golden stars looking unfamiliar and grouped in strange constellations. He was sure they were arranged in some order which had a secret and malign[19] significance. The wood on either side was full of singular noises, among which – once, twice, and again – he distinctly heard whispers in an unknown tongue.

His neck was in pain and lifting his hand to it he found it horribly swollen. He knew that it had a circle of black where the rope had bruised it. His eyes felt congested; he could no longer close them. His tongue was swollen with thirst; he relieved its fever by thrusting it forward from between his teeth into the cold air. How softly the turf had carpeted the untravelled avenue – he could no longer feel the roadway beneath his feet!

Doubtless, despite his suffering, he had fallen asleep while walking, for now he sees another scene – perhaps he has merely recovered from a delirium. He stands at the gate of his own home. All is as he left it, and all bright and beautiful in the morning sunshine. He must have travelled the entire night. As he pushes open the gate and passes up the wide white walk, he sees a flutter of female garments; his wife, looking fresh and cool and sweet, steps down from the veranda to meet him. At the bottom of the steps she stands waiting, with a smile of ineffable[20] joy, an attitude of matchless grace and dignity. Ah, how beautiful she is! He springs forward with extended arms. As he is about to clasp her he feels a stunning blow upon the back of the neck; a blinding white light blazes

---

[19] **malign:** threatening
[20] **ineffable:** unutterable

all about him with a sound like the shock of a cannon – then all is darkness and silence!

Peyton Farquhar was dead; his body, with a broken neck, swung gently from side to side beneath the timbers of the Owl Creek bridge. ◄

Activities

Close study (short story: narrative text)

1   Reread section II. Why was Farquhar so keen to support the Confederate (Southern) cause? How was he tricked by the Federal (Northern) scout?

2   Reread section I. How is Farquhar to be hanged from the bridge? How does the sound of the watch suggest time slowing? Of what does he dream as he waits?

3   Reread section III. What are the stages of Farquhar's apparent escape? What does he see and hear on the bank and in the river? What does he notice about the soldier shooting at him?

4   When he lands after being swept downstream, he looks at the beach and its surroundings. How does it appear to him?

5   What exactly are the blow and the blinding white light that end the vision of his return home to his wife?

Language study

6   The passage from 'All that day ... ' (page 43) to the end describes Farquhar's supposed final walk home to his plantation. It is really something he imagines just before the noose tightens. Find some words, phrases, sentences and comparisons that hint to us that this is not real experience.

7   Find some nouns, adjectives and adjectival phrases that create the beautiful last vision of his wife.

8   Why is there a gap after 'silence!' and why is the last paragraph so short?

Writing

9   'Nothing better exists,' wrote Stephen Crane, the novelist and storywriter. 'That story contains everything.' Write a review of what you find to enjoy in this story. You might like to include:
   • settings
   • main characters
   • storyline
   • technique, and use of flashback and shock
   • language contrasts
   • theme of a longing to live on in the face of death.

Reading

10   Other Civil War stories by Bierce that you might like to read include *The Coup de Grace*, *Chickamauga* and *One of the Missing*.

Resources

Websites styx.ios.com/~damone/gbierce.html

Pickets

Robert W. Chambers from *The Haunts of Men* (1898)

Robert W. Chambers (1865–1933) was a prolific American writer of best-selling novels, stories and nature books. Beginning as a magazine illustrator, he turned to writing, producing some eighty books in various genres. Perhaps he is best remembered for his supernatural tales, but this story, from The Haunts of Men *(1898), is well-known because an excellent film,* A Time Out of War, *was made from it.*

In this story, 'Pickets',[1] lonely sentries from the two sides in the Civil War face each other across a river in a quiet sector of the front. It is a hot day. They snipe at each other until they decide on a temporary truce.

'Hi, Yank!'

'Shut up!' replied Alden, wriggling to the edge of the rifle-pit. Connor also crawled a little higher and squinted through the chinks of the pine logs.

'Hey, Johnny!' he called across the river, 'are you that clay-eatin' Cracker with green lamps on your pilot?'

'Oh, Yank! Are yew the US[2] mewl with a CSA[3] brand on yewr head-stall?'

'Go to hell!' replied Connor sullenly.

A jeering laugh answered him from across the river.

'He had you there, Connor,' observed Alden with faint interest.

Connor took off his blue cap and examined the bullet hole in the crown.

'CSA brand on my head-stall, eh!' he repeated savagely, twirling the cap between his dirty fingers.

---

[1] **pickets:** sentries
[2] **US:** United States (North)
[3] **CSA:** Confederate States of America (South)

'You called him a clay-eating Cracker,' observed Alden; 'and you referred to his spectacles as green lanterns on his pilot.'

'I'll show him whose head-stall is branded,' muttered Connor, shoving his smoky rifle through the log crack.

Alden slid down to the bottom of the shallow pit and watched him apathetically.[4]

The silence was intense; the muddy river, smooth as oil, swirled noiselessly between its fringe of sycamores; not a breath of air stirred the leaves around them. From the sun-baked bottom of the rifle-pit came the stale smell of charred logs and smoke-soaked clothing. There was a stench of sweat in the air and the heavy odour of balsam and pine seemed to intensify it. Alden gasped once or twice, threw open his jacket at the throat, and stuffed a filthy handkerchief into the crown of his cap, arranging the ends as a shelter for his neck.

Connor lay silent, his right eye fastened upon the rifle-sight, his dusty army shoes crossed behind him. One yellow sock had slipped down over the worn shoe heel and laid bare a dust-begrimed ankle.

In the heated stillness Alden heard the boring of weevils in the logs overhead. A tiny twig snapped somewhere in the forest; a fly buzzed about his knees. Suddenly Connor's rifle cracked; the echoes rattled and clattered away through the woods; a thin cloud of pungent vapour slowly drifted straight upward, shredding into filmy streamers among the tangled branches overhead.

'Get him?' asked Alden, after a silence.

'Nope,' replied Connor. Then he addressed himself to his late target across the river:

'Hello, Johnny!'

'Hi, Yank!'

'How close?'

---

4 **apathetically:** without caring

'Hey?'

'How close?'

'What, sonny?'

'My shot, you fool!'

'Why, sonny!' called back the Confederate in affected surprise, 'was yew a shootin' at me?'

Bang! went Connor's rifle again. A derisive[5] cat-call answered him, and he turned furiously to Alden.

'Oh, let up,' said the young fellow; 'it's too hot for that.'

Connor was speechless with rage, and he hastily jammed another cartridge into his long, hot rifle, while Alden roused himself, brushed away a persistent fly, and crept up to the edge of the pit again.

'Hello, Johnny!' he shouted.

'That you, sonny?' replied the Confederate.

'Yes. Say, Johnny, shall we call it square until four o'clock?'

'What time is it?' replied the cautious Confederate; 'all our expensive gold watches is bein' repaired at Chickamauga.'[6]

At this taunt, Connor showed his teeth, but Alden laid one hand on his arm and sang out: 'It's two o'clock, Richmond[7] time; Sherman[8] has just telegraphed us from your State-house.'

'Wa-al, in that case this crool war is over,' replied the Confederate sharpshooter; 'we'll be easy on old Sherman.'

'See here!' cried Alden; 'is it a truce until four o'clock?'

'All right! Your word, Yank!'

'You have it!'

'Done!' said the Confederate, coolly rising to his feet and strolling down to the river bank, both hands in his pockets.

---

[5] **derisive:** mocking

[6] **Chickamauga:** site of the Southern battle success of 1863

[7] **Richmond:** Confederate capital

[8] **Sherman:** the Northern general

Alden and Connor crawled out of their ill-smelling dust wallow, leaving their rifles behind them.

'Whew! It's hot, Johnny,' said Alden pleasantly. He pulled out a stained pipe, blew into the stem, polished the bowl with his sleeve, and sucked wistfully at the end. Then he went and sat down beside Connor who had improvised a fishing pole from his ramrod, a bit of string and a rusty hook.

The Confederate rifleman also sat down on his side of the stream, puffing luxuriously on a fragrant corn-cob pipe.

Presently the Confederate soldier raised his head and looked across at Alden.

'What's yewr name, sonny?' he asked.

'Alden,' replied the young fellow briefly.

'Mine's Craig,' observed the Confederate; 'what's yewr regiment?'

'Two hundred sixtieth New York; what's yours, Mr Craig?'

'Ninety-third Maryland, *Mister* Alden.'

'Quit that throwin' sticks in the water!' growled Connor; 'how do you s'pose I'm goin' to catch anythin'?'

Alden tossed his stick back into the brush-heap and laughed.

'How's your tobacco, Craig?' he called out.

'Bully! How's yewr coffee 'n' tack,[9] Alden?'

'First-rate!' replied the youth.

After a silence he said: 'Is it a go?'

'You bet,' said Craig, fumbling in his pockets. He produced a heavy twist of Virginia tobacco, laid it on a log, hacked off about three inches with his sheath knife, and folded it up in a big green sycamore leaf. This again he rolled into a corn-husk, weighted with a pebble, then stepping back, he hurled it into the air, saying: 'Deal square, Yank!'

The tobacco fell at Alden's feet. He picked it up, measured it carefully with his clasp-knife, and called out: 'Three and three-quarters, Craig. What do you want, hard-tack or coffee?'

---

[9] **tack:** army biscuit

'Tack,' replied Craig; 'don't stint!'

Alden laid out two biscuits. As he was about to hack a quarter from the third he happened to glance over the creek at this enemy. There was no mistaking the expression in his face. Starvation was stamped on every feature.

When Craig caught Alden's eye, he spat with elaborate care, whistled a bar of the 'Bonny Blue Flag', and pretended to yawn.

Alden hesitated, glanced at Connor, then placed three whole biscuits in the corn husk, added a pinch of coffee, and tossed the parcel over to Craig.

That Craig longed to fling himself upon the food and devour it was plain to Alden, who was watching his face. But he didn't; he strolled leisurely down the bank, picked up the parcel, weighed it critically before opening it, and finally sat down to examine the contents. When he saw that the third cracker was whole, and that a pinch of coffee had been added, he paused in his examination and remained motionless on the bank, head bent. Presently he looked up and asked Alden if he had made a mistake. The young fellow shook his head and drew a long puff of smoke from his pipe, watching it curl out of his nose with interest.

'Then I'm obliged to yew, Alden,' said Craig; ''low, I'll eat a snack to see it ain't pizened.'

He filled his lean jaws with the dry biscuit, then scooped up a tin-cup full of water from the muddy river and set the rest of the cracker to soak.

'Good?' queried Alden.

'Fair,' drawled Craig, bolting an unchewed segment and choking a little. 'How's the twist?'

'Fine,' said Alden; 'tastes like stable-sweepings.'

They smiled at each other across the stream.

'Sa-a-y,' drawled Craig with his mouth full, 'when yew're out of twist, jest yew sing out, sonny.'

'All right,' replied Alden. He stretched back in the shadow of a sycamore and watched Craig with pleasant eyes.

Presently Connor had a bite and jerked his line into the air.

'Look yere,' said Craig, 'that ain't no way foh to ketch "red-horse". Yew want a ca'tridge on foh a sinker, sonny.'

'What's that?' inquired Connor suspiciously.

'Put on a sinker.'

'Go on, Connor,' said Alden.

Connor saw him smoking and sniffed anxiously. Alden tossed him the twist, telling him to fill his pipe.

Presently Connor found a small pebble and improvised a sinker. He swung his line again into the muddy current with a mechanical sidelong glance to see what Craig was doing, and settled down again on his haunches, smoking and grunting.

'Enny news, Alden?' queried Craig after a silence.

'Nothing much – except that Richmond has fallen,' grinned Alden.

'Quit foolin',' urged the Southerner; 'ain't thar no news?'

'No. Some of our men down at Long Pond got sick eating catfish. They caught them in the pond. It appears you Johnnys used the pond as a cemetery, and our men got sick eating the fish.'

'That so?' grinned Craig; 'too bad. Lots of yewr men was in Long Pond, too, I reckon.'

In the silence that followed, two rifle-shots sounded faint and dull from the distant forest.

''Nother great Union victory,' drawled Craig. 'Extry! extry! Richmond is took!'

Alden laughed and puffed at his pipe.

'We licked the boots off of the 30th Texas last Monday,' he said.

'Sho!' exclaimed Craig. 'What did you go a licking their boots for? – blackin'?'

'Oh, shut up!' said Connor from the bank, 'I can't ketch no fish if you two fools don't quit jawin'.'

The sun was dipping below the pine-clad ridge, flooding river and wood with a fierce radiance. The spruce needles glittered, edged with gold; every broad green leaf wore a heart of gilded splendour, and the muddy waters of the river rolled onward like a flood of precious metal, heavy, burnished, noiseless.

From a balsam bough a thrush uttered three timid notes; a great gauzy-winged grasshopper drifted blindly into a clump of sun-scorched weeds, click! click! cr-r-r-r!

'Purty,[10] ain't it,' said Craig, looking at the thrush. Then he swallowed the last morsel of muddy hard-tack, wiped his beard on his cuff, hitched up his trousers, took off his green glasses, and rubbed his eyes.

'A he-cat-bird sings purtier though,' he said with a yawn.

Alden drew out his watch, puffed once or twice, and stood up, stretching his arms in the air.

'It's four o'clock,' he began, but was cut short by a shout from Connor.

'Gee-whiz!' he yelled, 'what have I got on this here pole!'

The ramrod was bending, the line swaying heavily in the current.

'It's four o'clock, Connor,' said Alden, keeping a wary eye on Craig.

'That's all right!' called Craig; 'the time's extended till yewr friend lands that there fish!'

'Pulls like a porpoise,' grunted Connor, 'damn it! I bet it busts my ramrod!'

'Does it pull?' grinned Craig.

'Yes, – a dead weight!'

'Don't it jerk kinder this way an' that?' asked Craig, much interested.

'Naw,' said Connor, 'the bloody thing jest pulls steady.'

'Then it ain't no "red-horse", it's a catfish!'

'Huh!' sneered Connor, 'don't I know a catfish? This ain't no catfish, lemme tell yer!'

---

[10] **purty:** pretty

'Then it's a log,' laughed Alden.

'By gum! Here it comes,' panted Connor; 'here, Alden, jest you ketch it with my knife – hook the blade, blame ye!'

Alden cautiously descended the red bank of mud, holding on to roots and branches, and bent over the water. He hooked the big-bladed clasp knife like a scythe, set the spring, and leaned over the water.

'Now!' muttered Connor.

An oily circle appeared upon the surface of the turbid water – another and another. A few bubbles rose and floated upon the tide.

Then something black appeared just beneath the bubbles and Alden hooked it with his knife and dragged it shoreward.

It was the sleeve of a man's coat.

Connor dropped his ramrod and gaped at the thing: Alden would have loosed it, but the knife-blade was tangled in the sleeve.

He turned a sick face up to Connor.

'Pull it in,' said the older man, 'here, give it to me, lad –'.

When at last the silent visitor lay upon the bank, they saw it was the body of a Union[11] cavalryman. Alden stared at the dead face, fascinated; Connor mechanically counted the yellow chevrons upon the blue sleeve, now soaked black. The muddy water ran over the baked soil, spreading out in dust-covered pools; the spurred boots tricked slime. After a while both men turned their heads and looked at Craig. The Southerner stood silent and grave, his battered cap in his hand. They eyed each other quietly for a moment, then, with a vague gesture, the Southerner walked back into his pit and presently reappeared, trailing his rifle.

Connor had already begun to dig with his bayonet, but he glanced up at the rifle in Craig's hands. Then he looked suspiciously into the eyes of the Southerner. Presently he bent his head again and continued digging.

It was sunset before he and Alden finished the shallow grave, Craig

---

[11] **Union:** Northern army

watching them in silence, his rifle between his knees. When they were ready they rolled the body into the hole and stood up.

Craig also rose, raising his rifle to a 'present'.[12] He held it there while the two Union soldiers shovelled the earth into the grave. Alden went back and lifted the two rifles from the pit, handed Connor his, and waited.

'Ready!' growled Connor, 'aim!'

Alden's rifle came to his shoulder. Craig also raised his rifle.

'Fire!'

Three times the three shots rang out in the wilderness, over the unknown grave. After a moment or two Alden nodded good night to Craig across the river and walked slowly toward his rifle-pit. Connor shambled after him. As he turned to lower himself into the pit he called across the river; 'Good night, Craig!'

'Good night, Connor,' said Craig.

---

[12] **present:** military salute

Activities

Close study (short story: narrative text)

1   What are your impressions of the three soldiers, Connor and Alden (North) and Craig (South)? Mention their appearances, ages, ways of speaking and attitudes to each other.

2   Chambers describes the settings brilliantly. How does he use sensory detail in creating the atmosphere in:
    • the rifle pit
    • the river landscape?

3   The crisis of the story comes where Connor fishes up the dead Northern soldier:
    'It was the sleeve of a man's coat.'
    Why is this a single sentence paragraph? What further details of the dead man create horror and pity?

4   The story ends with the graveside rifle salute by all three soldiers. What is significant about the last exchange between Connor and Craig?

5   What is Chambers saying about the American Civil War in this vivid story?

Language study

6   Reread the section from ' "How's your tobacco?" ' (page 50) to ' ... with pleasant eyes.' (page 51) What do these short sentences from that section tell you about the characters?
    'Starvation was stamped on every feature.' (Craig)
    'He ... watched Craig with pleasant eyes.' (Alden)

7   What is the effect of these verbs connected with Craig?
    spat   whistled   pretended to yawn

8   Why say of Alden that he 'glanced at Connor' before he throws the food across?

9   What are the characters trying to do in these apparently hostile sentences?
    • 'I'll eat a snack to see it ain't pizened.'
    • '[The tobacco] tastes like stable-sweepings.'

Writing

10 Retell the story through the eyes of Craig. Mention the atmosphere of the hot day, the banter between the two sides, the exchange of food and tobacco and the chilling conclusion.

Reading

11 Other Civil War stories about broken friendships or relationships that you might like to read include *The Affair at Coulter's Neck* by Ambrose Bierce, *Three Miraculous Soldiers* and *The Little Regiment*, both by Stephen Crane.

A Night (Abridged)

Louisa May Alcott from *Hospital Sketches* (1863)

Louisa May Alcott (1832–1888) began to write in her teens. Her father's inability to provide for her mother and three sisters forced her into writing for a living. Fame and fortune came with Little Women *(1868), based on her own family upbringing in Concord, Massachusetts.*

The Alcotts, opposed to slavery, supported the Union's declaration of war in 1861. Alcott recorded her excitement: 'I like the stir in the air and long for battle, like a war horse when he smells powder'. In December, 1862, she answered an appeal for volunteer nurses. Her mother wrote 'Louisa goes into the very mouth of war' as her daughter went to work in a rough military hospital in Georgetown near Washington. Thousands of casualties from the bloody Battle of Fredericksburg overwhelmed the crude medical services. Treatment was rough. Walt Whitman, the poet, then a medical orderly in Washington, saw 'a heap of amputated feet, legs, arms, hands, etc., a full load for one horse cart'. Alcott's first grim task was to wash men whose wounds were caked in mud. She then found herself on the night shift in a maze of badly-ventilated, dimly-lit rooms. After three weeks of brave effort, she became severely ill with typhoid fever, and returned home.

When she recovered, she used her diary and letters home to compose Hospital Sketches *(1863), calling herself 'Nurse Tribulation Periwinkle' and toning down the horrors she had seen. Most admired was 'A Night' with its sad picture of the death of John Sulie, a Virginian blacksmith, 'into which,' wrote a reviewer, 'it was plain she had put her whole heart'.*

Being fond of the night side of nature, I was soon promoted to the post of night nurse, with every facility for indulging in my favourite pastime of 'owling'.[1] My colleague, a black-eyed widow, relieved me at dawn, we two taking care of the ward between us, like regular nurses, turn and turn about. I usually found my boys in the jolliest state of mind their condition allowed; for it was a known fact that Nurse Periwinkle objected to blue devils,[2] and entertained a belief that he who laughed most was surest of recovery. At the beginning of my reign, dumps and dismals prevailed; the nurses looked anxious and tired, the men gloomy or sad; and a general 'Hark! from-the-tombs-a-doleful-sound' style of conversation seemed to be the fashion: a state of things which caused one coming from a merry, social New England town, to feel as if she had got into an exhausted receiver;[3] and the instinct of self-preservation, to say nothing of philanthropic desire[4] to serve the race, caused a speedy change in Ward No. I.

More flattering than the most gracefully turned compliment, more grateful that the most admiring glance, was the sight of those rows of faces, all strange to me a little while ago, now lighting up, with smiles of welcome, as I came among them, enjoying that moment heartily, with a womanly pride in their regard, a motherly affection for them all. The evenings were spent in reading aloud, writing letters, waiting on and amusing the men, going the rounds with Dr P., as he made his second daily survey, dressing my dozen wounds afresh, giving last doses, and making them cosy for the long hours to come, till the nine o'clock bell rang, the gas was turned down, the day nurses went off duty, the night watch came on, and my nocturnal[5] adventures began.

My ward was now divided into three rooms; and, under favour of the matron, I had managed to sort out the patients in such a way that I had what I called, my 'duty room', my 'pleasure room', and my 'pathetic

[1] **owling:** working at night
[2] **blue devils:** depression
[3] **receiver:** a glass jar with no air in it
[4] **philanthropic desire:** the wish to do good
[5] **nocturnal:** night time

room', and worked for each in a different way. One, I visited, armed with a dressing tray, full of rollers,[6] plasters and pins; another, with books, flowers, games and gossip; a third, with teapots, lullabies, consolation, and, sometimes, a shroud.

'John is going, ma'am, and wants to see you if you can come.'

'The moment this boy is asleep; tell him so, and let me know if I am in danger of being too late.'

My Ganymede[7] departed, and while I quieted poor Shaw, I thought of John. He came in a day or two after the others; and, one evening, when I entered my 'pathetic room', I found a lately emptied bed occupied by a large, fair man, with a fine face, and the serenest eyes I ever met. One of the earlier comers had often spoken of a friend, who had remained behind, that those apparently worse wounded than himself might reach a shelter first. It seemed a David and Jonathan[8] sort of friendship. The man fretted for his mate, and was never tired of praising John – his courage, sobriety, self-denial, and unfailing kindliness of heart; always winding up with: 'He's an out an' out fine feller, ma'am; you see if he ain't'.

I had some curiosity to behold this piece of excellence, and when he came, watched him for a night or two, before I made friends with him; for, to tell the truth, I was a little afraid of the stately looking man, whose bed had to be lengthened to accommodate his commanding stature; who seldom spoke, uttered no complaint, asked no sympathy, but tranquilly observed what went on about him; and, as he lay high upon his pillows, no picture of dying statesman or warrior was ever fuller of real dignity than this Virginia blacksmith. A most attractive face he had, framed in brown hair and beard, comely featured and full of vigour, as yet unsubdued by pain; thoughtful and often beautifully mild while watching the afflictions

---

[6] **rollers:** bandages

[7] **Ganymede:** messenger

[8] **David and Jonathan:** famous Biblical friendship

of others, as if entirely forgetful of his own. His mouth was grave and firm, with plenty of will and courage in its lines, but a smile could make it as sweet as any woman's; and his eyes were child's eyes, looking one fairly in the face, with a clear, straightforward glance, which promised well for such as placed their faith in him. He seemed to cling to life, as if it were rich in duties and delights, and he had learned the secret of content. The only time I saw his composure disturbed, was when my surgeon brought another to examine John, who scrutinised their faces with an anxious look, asking of the elder: 'Do you think I shall pull through, sir?' 'I hope so, my man.' And, as the two passed on, John's eye still followed them, with an intentness which would have won a truer answer from them, had they seen it. A momentary shadow flitted over his face; then came the usual serenity, as if, in that brief eclipse, he had acknowledged the existence of some hard possibility, and, asking nothing yet hoping all things, left the issue in God's hands, with that submission which is true piety.

The next night, as I went my rounds with Dr P., I happened to ask which man in the room probably suffered most; and, to my great surprise, he glanced at John:

'Every breath he draws is like a stab; for the ball pierced the left lung, broke a rib, and did no end of damage here and there; so the poor lad can find neither forgetfulness nor ease, because he must lie on his wounded back or suffocate. It will be a hard struggle, and a long one, for he possesses great vitality; but even his temperate life can't save him; I wish it could.'

'You don't mean he must die, Doctor?'

'Bless you, there's not the slightest hope for him; and you'd better tell him so before long; women have a way of doing such things comfortably, so I leave it to you. He won't last more than a day or two, at furthest.'

I could have sat down on the spot and cried heartily, if I had not learned the wisdom of bottling up one's tears for leisure moments. Such an end seemed very hard for such a man, when half a dozen worn out, worthless bodies round him, were gathering up the remnants of wasted lives, to linger on for years perhaps, burdens to others, daily reproaches to themselves. The army needed men like John, earnest, brave, and faithful; fighting for liberty and justice with both heart and hand, true soldiers of the Lord. I could not give him up so soon, or think with any patience of so excellent a nature robbed of its fulfilment, and blundered into eternity by the rashness or stupidity of those at whose hands so many lives may be required. It was an easy thing for Dr P. to say: 'Tell him he must die,' but a cruelly hard thing to do, and by no means as 'comfortable' as he politely suggested. I had not the heart to do it then, and privately indulged the hope that some change for the better might take place, in spite of gloomy prophesies; so, rendering my task unnecessary.

A few minutes later, as I came in again, with fresh rollers, I saw John sitting erect, with no one to support him, while the surgeon dressed his back. I had never hitherto seen it done; for, having simpler wounds to attend to, and knowing the fidelity of the attendant, I had left John to him, thinking it might be more agreeable and safe; for both strength and experience were needed in his case. I had forgotten that the strong man might long for the gentle tendance of a woman's hands, the sympathetic magnetism of a woman's presence, as well as the feebler souls about him. The Doctor's words caused me to reproach myself with neglect, not of any real duty perhaps, but of those little cares and kindnesses that solace homesick spirits, and make the heavy hours pass easier. John looked lonely and forsaken just then, as he sat with bent head, hands folded on his knee, and no outward sign of suffering, till, looking nearer, I saw great tears roll down and drop upon the floor. It was a new sight there; for, though I had seen many suffer, some swore, some groaned, most endured silently, but none wept. Yet it did not seem weak, only very touching, and straightway my fear vanished, my heart opened wide and took him in, as, gathering the bent head in my arms, as freely as if he had been a little child, I said, 'Let me help you bear it, John.'

Never, on any human countenance, have I seen so swift and beautiful a look of gratitude, surprise and comfort, as that which answered me
more eloquently[9] than the whispered –

'Thank you, ma'am, this is right good! This is what I wanted!'

'Then why not ask for it before?'

'I didn't like to be a trouble; you seemed so busy, and I could manage
to get on alone.'

'You shall not want it any more, John.'

Nor did he; for now I understood the wistful look that sometimes
followed me, as I went out, after a brief pause beside his bed, or merely a
passing nod, while busied with those who seemed to need me more
than he, because more urgent in their demands. Now I knew that to him,
as to so many, I was the poor substitute for mother, wife, or sister, and in
his eyes no stranger, but a friend who hitherto had seemed neglectful;
for, in his modesty, he had never guessed the truth. This was changed
now; and, through the tedious operation of probing, bathing, and dressing his wounds, he leaned against me, holding my hand fast, and, if pain
wrung further tears from him, no one saw them fall but me. When he
was laid down again, I hovered about him, in a remorseful state of mind
that would not let me rest, till I had bathed his face, brushed his bonny
brown hair, set all things smooth about him, and laid a knot of heath and
heliotrope on his clean pillow. While doing this, he watched me with the
satisfied expression I so liked to see; and when I offered the little
nosegay, held it carefully in his great hand, smoothed a ruffled leaf or
two, surveyed and smelt it with an air of genuine delight, and lay
contentedly regarding the glimmer of the sunshine on the green.
Although the manliest man among my forty, he said 'Yes, ma'am,' like a
little boy; received suggestions for his comfort with the quick smile that
brightened his whole face; and now and then, as I stood tidying the table

---

[9] **eloquently:** fluently and clearly

by his bed, I felt him softly touch my gown, as if to assure himself that I was there. Anything more natural and frank I never saw, and found this brave John as bashful as brave, yet full of excellencies and fine aspirations, which, having no power to express themselves in words, seemed to have bloomed into his character and made him what he was.

After that night, an hour of each evening that remained to him was devoted to his ease or pleasure. He could not talk much, for breath was precious, and he spoke in whispers; but from occasional conversations, I gleaned scraps of private history which only added to the affection and respect I felt for him. Once he asked me to write a letter, and as I settled pen and paper, I said, with an irrepressible glimmer of feminine curiosity, 'Shall it be addressed to wife, or mother, John?'

'Neither, ma'am; I've got no wife, and will write to mother myself when I get better. Did you think I was married because of this?' he asked, touching a plain ring he wore, and often turned thoughtfully on his finger when he lay alone.

'Partly that, but more from a settled sort of look you have; a look which young men seldom get until they marry.'

'I didn't know that; but I'm not so very young, ma'am, thirty in May, and have been what you might call settled this ten years. Mother's a widow, I'm the oldest child she has, and it wouldn't do for me to marry until Lizzy has a home of her own, and Jack's learned his trade; for we're not rich, and I must be father to the children and husband to the dear old woman, if I can.'

'No doubt but you are both, John; yet how came you to go to war, if you felt so? Wasn't enlisting as bad as marrying?'

'No, ma'am, not as I see it, for one is helping my neighbour, the other pleasing myself. I went because I couldn't help it. I didn't want the glory or the pay; I wanted the right thing done, and people kept saying the men who were in earnest ought to fight. I was in earnest, the Lord knows! but I held off as long as I could, not knowing which was my duty. Mother saw the case, gave me her ring to keep me steady, and said "Go": so I went.'

A short story and a simple one, but the man and the mother were portrayed better than pages of fine writing could have done it.

'Do you ever regret that you came, when you lie here suffering so much?'

'Never, ma'am; I haven't helped a great deal, but I've shown I was willing to give my life, and perhaps I've got to; but I don't blame anybody, and if it was to do over again, I'd do it. I'm a little sorry I wasn't wounded in front; it looks cowardly to be hit in the back, but I obeyed orders, and it don't matter in the end, I know.'

Poor John! it did not matter now, except that a shot in front might have spared the long agony in store for him. He seemed to read the thought that troubled me, as he spoke so hopefully when there was no hope, for he suddenly added:

'This is my first battle; do they think it's going to be my last?'

'I'm afraid they do, John.'

It was the hardest question I had ever been called upon to answer; doubly hard with those clear eyes fixed on mine, forcing a truthful answer by their own truth. He seemed a little startled at first, pondered over the fateful fact a moment, then shook his head, with a glance at the broad chest and muscular limbs stretched out before him:

'I'm not afraid, but it's difficult to believe all at once. I'm so strong it don't seem possible for such a little wound to kill me.'

Merry Mercutio's[10] dying words glanced through my memory as he spoke: ''Tis not so deep as a well nor so wide as a church door, but 'tis enough'. And John would have said the same could he have seen the ominous black holes between his shoulders; he never had, but, seeing the ghastly sights about him, could not believe his own wound more fatal than these, for all the suffering it caused him.

[10] **Mercutio:** a character in *Romeo and Juliet* by William Shakespeare

'Shall I write to your mother, now?' I asked, thinking that these sudden tidings might change all plans and purposes. But they did not; for the man received the order of the Divine Commander to march with the same unquestioning obedience with which the soldier had received that of the human one; doubtless remembering that the first led him to life, and the last to death.

'No, ma'am; to Jack just the same; he'll break it to her best, and I'll add a line to her myself when you get done.'

So I wrote the letter which he dictated, finding it better than any I had sent; for, though here and there a little ungrammatical or inelegant, each sentence came to me briefly worded, but most expressive; full of excellent counsel to the boy, tenderly bequeathing 'mother and Lizzie' to his care, and bidding him good bye in words the sadder for their simplicity. He added a few lines, with steady hand, and, as I sealed it, said, with a patient sort of sigh, 'I hope the answer will come in time for me to see it'; then, turning away his face, laid the flowers against his lips, as if to hide some quiver of emotion at the thought of such a sudden sundering[11] of all the dear home ties.

These things had happened two days before; now John was dying, and the letter had not come. I had been summoned to many death beds in my life, but to none that made my heart ache as it did then, since my mother called me to watch the departure of a spirit akin to[12] this in its gentleness and patient strength. As I went in, John stretched out both hands:

'I knew you'd come! I guess I'm moving on, ma'am.'

He was; and so rapidly that, even while he spoke, over his face I saw the grey veil falling that no human hand can lift. I sat down by him, wiped the drops from his forehead, stirred the air about him with the slow wave of a fan, and waited to help him die. He stood in sore need of

---

[11] **sundering:** breaking
[12] **akin to:** like

help – and I could do so little; for, as the doctor had foretold, the strong body rebelled against death, and fought every inch of the way, forcing him to draw each breath with a spasm, and clench his hands with an imploring look, as if he asked, 'How long must I endure this, and be still!' For hours he suffered dumbly, without a moment's respite, or a moment's murmuring, his limbs grew cold, his face damp, his lips white and, again and again, he tore the covering off his breast, as if the lightest weight added to his agony; yet through it all, his eyes never lost their perfect serenity, and the man's soul seemed to sit therein, undaunted by the ills that vexed his flesh.

One by one, the men woke, and round the room appeared a circle of pale faces and watchful eyes, full of awe and pity; for, though a stranger, John was beloved by all. Each man there had wondered at his patience, respected his piety, admired his fortitude, and now lamented his hard death; for the influence of an upright nature had made itself deeply felt, even in one little week. Presently, the Jonathan who so loved this comely David, came creeping from his bed for a last look and word. The kind soul was full of trouble, as the choke in his voice, the grasp of his hand, betrayed; but there were no tears, and the farewell of the friends was the more touching for its brevity.

'Old boy, how are you?' faltered the one.

'Most through, thank heaven!' whispered the other.

'Can I say or do anything for you anywheres?'

'Take my things home, and tell them that I did my best.'

'I will! I will!'

'Good bye, Ned!'

'Good bye, John, good bye!'

They kissed each other, tenderly as women, and so parted, for poor Ned could not stay to see his comrade die. For a little while, there was no sound in the room but the drip of water, from a stump or two, and John's distressful gasps, as he slowly breathed his life away. I thought him nearly gone, and had just laid down the fan, believing its help to be no longer needed, when suddenly he rose up in his bed, and cried out with a bitter cry that broke the silence, sharply startling every one with its agonised appeal:

'For God's sake, give me air!'

It was the only cry pain or death had wrung from him, the only boon[13] he had asked; and none of us could grant it, for all the airs that blew were useless now. Dan flung up the window. The first red streak of dawn was warming the grey east, a herald of the coming sun; John saw it, and with the love of light which lingers in us to the end, seemed to read in it a sign of hope of help, for, over his whole face there broke that mysterious expression, brighter than any smile, which often comes to eyes that look their last. He laid himself gently down; and, stretching out his strong right arm, as if to grasp and bring the blessed air to his lips in a fuller flow, lapsed into a merciful unconsciousness, which assured us that for him suffering was forever past. He died then; for, though the heavy breaths still tore their way up for a little longer, they were but the waves of an ebbing tide that beat unfelt against the wreck, which an immortal voyager had deserted with a smile. He never spoke again, but to the end held my hand close, so close that when he was asleep at last, I could not draw it away. Dan helped me, warning me as he did so that it was unsafe for dead and living flesh to lie so long together; but though my hand was strangely cold and stiff, and four white marks remained across its back, even when warmth and colour had returned elsewhere, I could not but be glad that, through its touch, the presence of human sympathy, perhaps, had lightened that hard hour.

When they had made him ready for the grave, John lay in state for half an hour, a thing which seldom happened in that busy place; but a universal sentiment of reverence and affection seemed to fill the hearts of all

---

[13] **boon:** favour

who had known or heard of him; and when the rumour of his death went through the house, always astir, many came to see him, and I felt a tender sort of pride in my lost patient; for he looked a most heroic figure, lying there stately and still as the statue of some young knight asleep upon his tomb. The lovely expression which so often beautifies dead faces, soon replaced the marks of pain, and I longed for those who loved him best to see him when half an hour's acquaintance with Death had made them friends. As we stood looking at him, the ward master handed me a letter, saying it had been forgotten the night before. It was John's letter, come just an hour too late to gladden the eyes that had longed and looked for it so eagerly! but he had it; for, after I had cut some brown locks for his mother, and taken off the ring to send her, telling how well the talisman[14] had done its work, I kissed this good son for her sake, and laid the letter in his hand, still folded as when I drew my own away, feeling that its place was there, and making myself happy with the thought, that, even in his solitary grave in the 'Government Lot', he would not be without some token of the love which makes life beautiful and outlives death. Then I left him, glad to have known so genuine a man, and carrying with me an enduring memory of the brave Virginia blacksmith, as he lay serenely waiting for the dawn of that long day which knows no night. ◀

---

[14] ***talisman:*** lucky token

Activities

Close study (fiction based on letters/journal: recount text)

1 What are the narrator's duties at the hospital each day? What does she emphasise in her approach?

2 How does she feel about her task of telling John that he is dying? In what ways does she try to help him as a nurse? Which are the most touching features of his response?

3 What do we learn of John's background and motives for joining the army? What is in the last letter to Jack?

4 What is moving and terrible about John's death? Why mention the sunrise?

5 How does the answer to the letter add to the drama?

6 How does the nurse try to help John's family after his death?

7 What are her thoughts about the war and about John's death in it?

Language study

8 Reread the section from 'He was; and so rapidly ... ' (page 65) to the end. Alcott uses several metaphors (indirect comparisons) and similes (direct comparisons) to describe John's death. What is compared to what in each?

9 Although not as sentimental as other Civil War nursing memoirs (''tis a privilege even thus to die for one's country'), Alcott cannot escape the style of the time. Find some examples of overdone emotion in the passage.

10 On the other hand, Alcott can be blunt and truthful. John's last shouted words are an example. Find other examples of grim reality.

Writing

11 Compose the letter that the nurse might have written to John's mother about his part in the war and about his death.

12 Read 'Ambulance Train' by Helen Zenna Smith (page 94), also about women's work in wartime. Compare it with 'A Night', considering:
- the nature of the work
- the attitude to war
- the pictures of war's victims
- the language.

Reading

13 You might like to read the other *Hospital Sketches* by Louisa May Alcott, and Walt Whitman's poems on his work as a medical orderly: 'A Sight in Camp', 'The Wound-Dresser' and 'Vigil Strange'.

Resources

Websites www.alcottweb.com/
www.louisamayalcott.org

Boer War (1899–1902)

The Boers, descended from Dutch settlers in South Africa, resented British claims to the gold-rich province of Transvaal. The Boers invaded Natal and Cape Colony, enjoying early successes in battle. The British victory at Paardeberg Drift in 1900 was decisive. The subsequent Boer guerrilla campaign was crushed by General Kitchener's 'scorched earth' policy that burned Boer farms and detained women and children in internment camps. Around 20,000 people in these camps died from disease and neglect.

Resources for pages 70–77

Books *The Boer War* by Tabitha Jackson
Videos *The Boer War* by Cromwell Productions
Websites www.anglo.boer.co.za/
www.national.army.museum.ac.uk

Previously Unreported

Edgar Wallace from *Unofficial Despatches* (1901)

*Edgar Wallace (1875–1932) escaped from a poor London background
when he joined the army. After training as a medical orderly, he was sent
to South Africa before the Boer War started. There he discovered a gift for
writing, and submitted poems to local journals. He left the army but
became a war correspondent when fighting began in 1899. He toured the
veldt on a bicycle, looking for stories and sometimes helping army
surgeons. 'I am seeing life,' he told a friend, 'and God knows a fair share
of death.'*

*His reports for the Daily Mail aroused interest and even controversy.
Sometimes he sent them home in code to avoid censorship. They were
published as* Unofficial Despatches *in 1901, at the same time as his
collection of war poetry,* Writ in Barracks. *His writing was admired as
'very, very human ... the sort of thing that will go home to men's hearts'.*

*Wallace, like the poet, Rudyard Kipling, respected 'Tommy Atkins',
the ordinary British soldier, whose status had been unjustly low in the
Victorian era. In* Previously Unreported, *he arouses the reader's pity for
the lonely fate of a young soldier who represents many others. He wants
us to understand the meaning of the stark military word 'unreported':
that a man can be shot down and lost in the vastness of the South
African bush.*

Because there are so many Jim Burtons, and have been, I tell you this.

It explains better than most ways one of the many things people
cannot understand.

You cannot understand why we don't catch De Wet[1] or why we don't
smash Botha,[1] or what we are doing with the thousands of troops in

---

[1] **De Wet/Botha:** Dutch generals

South Africa, or why there are fifty places out here called Graspan, and a hundred Spion Kops, and Heaven knows how many Kalkfonteins; and you don't know why, on May 14th, appears on page 2 of the *Daily Mail*, under 'Casualties in South Africa', the announcement: 'Previously unreported. – Private T. Atkins, killed in engagement at Warm Baths, December 4th, 1900'.

Jim Burton – his name wasn't Jim Burton at all, but I just call him that – was a case you would also find it difficult to understand, so I make a little story of it because, being true, not only of his case but of hundreds of others, you would vote it dreary, since truth is duller than fiction; or else refuse to believe it at all.

First of all, Jim Burton's home. The straggling street in a village between Maidstone and Rochester is made up of many such houses as Jim Burton's. No uniformity attempted, for the cottages were built before the days of parish councils, and before the dictum[2] of committees of architecture condemned rural builders to cultivate sanitary unloveliness. Here in the broad street or on the unkempt reaches of commonage Jim Burton played, and in the half-acre ' 'lotment' near to Widow Burton's cottage Jim Burton, as a boy, worked o' evenings – wearisome, back-aching half hours unrighteously stolen from his play-time, and resented as such. Here, in this well-ordered, lightly-packed patch of ripening green and mellowing gold, Jim planted and hoed and dug and cut. Widow Burton's cottage stands back from the road, and is reached by a cobble-covered pathway flanked in due season by tall hollyhocks, and the door and windows of the thatch-roofed dwelling are half hidden behind the festoons of climbing roses that droop from the covered wall. Inside the cottage dust is not, nor disorder, nor tarnish. The furniture shines, the brasses glow, and the tin canisters on the mantelshelf over the high, deep fireplace positively glare.

---

[2] **dictum:** order

Jim knew those tins; they were a grievance in the same category as gardening; and on the injustice of being forced to polish them daily, so that they won approval from a critical mother – no easy task that, either – he was wont to brood darkly. Perhaps it was those tins that suggested in his youthful heart the possibilities of soldiering as a profession, as an alternative to this domestic slavery, for Jim was at the age when boys dream of Great Glory – nor do they wash their necks.

In the parlour, with its grim horse-hair suite – the gift of Grandmother Burton, long gone to rest and buried in Buckinghamshire, or some such foreign place – the hundred years old clock stands sentry over the alcove in which Grandmother Burton's old china is laid away.

On the table – a loo table,[3] cloth covered and set around with books at painfully regular intervals – is Jim's portrait in the uniform of the 50th Queen's Own Royal West Kent Regiment. Not an unpleasing face; hair parted in the middle, with a huge curl plastered flat on the forehead.

Jim spent two hours over that curl the afternoon he was 'took' – a very serious afternoon, big with event, and lightened only by the facetious observation addressed to the Maidstone photographer, 'Mind my fice don't break your camera,' for Jim had dropped his Kentish accent, and had adopted that of the delightful Deptford cockneys forming the bulk of his brave old regiment.

I could tell you of Widow Burton, but you have seen hundreds of such women; seen them in the winter shawl clad by their firesides, dozing back into the long dead years, conjuring back faces that do not bear the seams of age, and raising to the quick[4] people who are so many names on moss-covered stones. You have seen her like in the summer, sitting by the porch with folded arms, content and placid, and taking in new life with the warm young air and the sweet faint scents; there

---

[3] *loo table:* card table
[4] *raising to the quick:* bringing to life

among the flowers she sits, rare old gold, chaste and chastened among a thousand uncut gems.

I could tell you of many things that would weary you. Of Jim's girl, of Jim's dog, lurching disconsolately around familiar haunts; of Jim's old gun rusting on the wall; of the schemes that flit through Widow Burton's mind for Jim's welfare what time he leaves the Army; but home, hopes, mother, garden, girl and dog – they were all Jim's.

Ten miles from Enslin, on the road to Klip Drift, we English fought a running fight with a small detached commando of the invaders. That was three months ago. Widow Burton doesn't know that, for she does not read the newspapers, and nobody has told her, not even the War Office, for Jim had been detached from his regiment, and his CO wasn't quite certain whether Jim was acting as orderly to a general at the base or signaller to a flying column.[5] As a matter of fact, he had joined a column – the column that had the fight – the morning it moved out, and in consequence was not inscribed on the nominal roll.[6] It is a wild, weird place, this Rooilaagte, where the fight was, and there are several neat little mounds of earth with rude crosses bearing the names of the men who fell and their regiments.

Jim's is not one of these. Three miles to the right of the Boers' central position is a little kloof – a narrow bush-grown opening between two kopjes[7] falling sheer. In such a place a man might be easily sniped, and no one be any the wiser, especially if he was not missed except by a widow, who would fall to speculating why a letter did not come.

Here, where the grasses are thickest and the bushes more entangled, lies a man.

---

[5] **flying column:** a group of fast-moving horsemen
[6] **nominal roll:** list of names
[7] **kopjes:** hills

His face is to the ground and cannot be seen, which is well, for it is not good to look upon.

A little lizard basking on one sun-bathed patch of rock, twisting its head, looks curiously; a herd of buck, pattering timorously past, stops and gazes fearfully.

Be curious, little lizard, this boy will throw no more stones; fear nothing, you round-eyed, graceful creatures, the hunter's gun is resting in Kent, and that which he holds in shrunken, grey fingers he cannot use.

Activities

Close study (non-fiction journalism: recount text)

1 What do you know of Jim's upbringing? Which details show that the author admires the Burtons' way of life?
2 Why did Jim join the army? What does Wallace think of the army? (He, like Jim, had joined the Royal West Kent Regiment.)
3 What do we learn about Widow Burton? How does Wallace make us feel sympathy for her?
4 The story cuts dramatically to South Africa. How do the place names and the description of the landscape and its creatures make it seem alien?
5 How exactly was Jim killed and then forgotten?

Language study

6 Other writers worried about the deaths of brave, simple soldiers who died in wars they did not understand. Thomas Hardy read about the death of a drummer boy from Dorset. He wrote this poem about him.

Drummer Hodge

They throw in Drummer Hodge to rest
    Uncoffined – just as found:
His landmark is a kopje crest
    That breaks the veldt around;
And foreign constellations west
    Each night above his mound.

Young Hodge the Drummer never knew –
    Fresh from his Wessex home –
The meaning of the broad Karoo,
    The Bush, the dusty loam,
And why uprose to nightly view
    Strange stars amid the gloam.

Yet portion of that unknown plain
    Will Hodge forever be;
His homely Northern breast and brain
    Grow to some Southern tree,
And strange-eyed constellations reign
    His stars eternally.

7 Compare the story and poem, considering:
- how the young men are portrayed
- how their fates are described
- how the South African landscape and fauna are used
- the messages about war.

Reading

8 Other poems by Thomas Hardy on the Boer War that you might like to read include 'A Wife in London', 'The Colonel's Soliloquy', 'A Christmas Ghost Story', 'Horses Aboard' and 'The Man He Killed'.

First World War (1914–1918)

Tensions among the great European powers – based on political, territorial and colonial rivalries – had been rising since the turn of the century. Balkan nationalism produced a flash point at Sarajevo in Bosnia in June, 1914. By August, two great alliances – Britain and her Empire, France, Russia and Italy, and Germany, Austria-Hungary and Turkey – were at war.

On the Eastern Front, a fluid conflict of Germans, Austro-Hungarians and Russians caused massive casualties and the eventual collapse of Russia into revolution in 1917. On the Western Front, the war took its characteristic and best remembered shape: heavily defended trench lines which produced deadlock and, in nightmarish battles of 'attrition', like Verdun and the Somme (1916) or Ypres (1917), enormous numbers of dead and wounded.

The Germans broke the Western Front in March 1918, but the Anglo-French counter-attack, supported by the Americans, who joined the war in April 1917, finally defeated the Germans by November 1918.

Resources for pages 78–102

Books *The First World War* by Martin Gilbert
  1914–18: The Great War by Jay Winter
Videos *1914–18: Total War – The Crucible* by BBC
  War in the Trenches and *The Great War* both by Cromwell Productions
Websites www.iwm.org.uk
  www.bbc.co.uk/history/wwone
  www.worldwar1.com/
  www.spartacus.schoolnet.co.uk/FWWtrench.htm

A Battlepiece (Abridged)

Frederick Britten Austin from *When the War God Walks Again* (1926)

Frederick Britten Austin (1885–1941) was a successful popular author and playwright. He enlisted on 4 August, 1914, when war began, and served as an officer for several years in France and Flanders.

'A Battlepiece', published in 1926, looks back on the horrors of trench warfare. Britten describes a nightmare attack, probably at Ypres, in 1917. Even tanks and low-flying aircraft cannot help the infantry, fighting in a wasteland of 'very fluid' mud.

Like many ex-soldiers, Britten resented the military high command that planned and ran the great Western Front offensives. These officers, whose hats and collars were red-tabbed, worked far away from the fighting. Philip Gibbs, a journalist, watched them at Army Headquarters in Montreuil:

> *Often one saw the Commander-in-chief starting for an afternoon ride, a fine figure, nobly mounted with an escort of Lancers ... a pretty sight, with fluttering pennons on all their lances ... Such careless-hearted courage when British soldiers were being blown to bits, gassed, blinded, maimed, and shell-shocked in places that were far – so very far – from GHQ!*

Realities of War (1929)

▶ That, gentleman, will conclude the first phase of the attack. The brigade will then press on, at all costs –'

The officers of four battalions filled the large barn. It was illumined, through the wide-open great doors in its flank, in a cool reflection of the blaze of hot summer sunshine outside. At the further end, on chairs brought from the farmhouse, sat the red-tabbed Brigadier, the red-tabbed

Brigade-Major, the four Colonels and their four Seconds-in-Command. Among them, erect, stood another red-tabbed staff officer, middle-aged, tall, precise-mannered, with an air of authority and the rank of Lieutenant-Colonel. In front of him, a table supported a large relief-model of a section of country scriggled over with red and blue lines. Behind him, on the wall of the barn, was a large map similarly reticulated.[1] As he talked, he emphasised his points with a thrust of his cane to various features of the map and the relief-model 'which he hoped all would presently come forward and study with the utmost care'.

The infantry officers, in a curious mixture of ages that did not at all tally with their ranks, stood closely grouped or found precarious seats on such agricultural implements as had been left in the barn. There was a curious nervous tension in the silence with which they listened. And not without cause. They were listening to what, for an unknown percentage of them, was a sentence of certain death. No one voiced that aspect of the matter. A psychological X-ray would have revealed each one resolutely suppressing any personal thought, focussing his attention on the technicalities being expounded to them, and attuning himself stoically to the unemotional professionalism of the tall, neatly-uniformed, awkwardly-spoken staff officer. There was going to be another 'push'.[2] Here, in this peaceful back area of ancient farmhouses embosomed in full-grown summer verdure where the Divisions had, in cynical mess-parlance,[3] been 'fattened for the slaughter', the high gods of the 'Army' staff, having duly impressed upon the Corps Staffs and the Divisional Staffs what was expected of them, had condescended to explain their requirements, in a series of 'Brigade Conferences', to the people who would actually do the work. That humble, lowest-paid arm of the service which throughout the army had succinctly become known as the PBI – translatable for delicate ears as 'Poor Blooming

---

[1]   **reticulated:** marked with lines
[2]   **push:** huge attack
[3]   **parlance:** way of talking

Infantry' – should in consequence go forth to battle inspired to Berserk[4]-ecstasy in that matter of close-quarter killing and dying which was its interesting prerogative.

Bitterly although every infantry officer in that barn hated the Staff – with a hatred far transcending any they felt for the enemy – they nevertheless listened with an instinctive awe. It was an awe for which every infantry subaltern[5] in the army kicked himself and yet to which he could not succumb. That symbol of red-tabs on the lapels and a red band round the cap was so manifestly the symbol of a superior race. On those who wore it the gods had conferred immortality as well as authority. None of them would be killed, except by accident. Few of them had spent a night in the open since the war began. It was rumoured that some of them even dressed for dinner every evening. And on the intermittent occasions when they were seen in the squalor of the trenches, for sojourns of the briefest possible duration, they had – awkward in rarely-worn steel helmets and concerned about the mud on their nicely-polished leggings – irresistibly the air of aristocratic philanthropists[6] visiting the slums. Even hard-faced infantry colonels of long and arduous service became soft-spoken and polite when addressed by some second lieutenant ADC wearing that mystic colour. The prestige of it was irresistible. It betokened membership of the sacred caste to whom war was a matter of poring over maps or signing endless floods of paper – who could, and did, release with a word (written cigarette in mouth in a quiet office), a fury of annihilating forces from whose destructiveness they themselves were happily exempt. They listened therefore to the staff officer at the table – he was GSO 2 at Army Headquarters and had a reputation for being uncommonly efficient.

He concluded his remarks.

---

[4] **Berserk:** wild, out of control
[5] **subaltern:** junior officer
[6] **philanthropists:** people who do good

' ... Co-operation with the other arms – tanks, artillery and aircraft – will be as nearly perfect as we can get it. I need not tell you that. But I need not tell you either that it is on the infantry that all finally depends – it must advance with unflinching determination, regardless of its losses –'

'Poor b— infantry again!' murmured a disillusioned youthful subaltern in the throng. 'All the kicks – and no ruddy ha'pence!'

The staff officer picked up his gloves from the table. He would have scorned to be an orator,[7] and winding up a speech was even more difficult to him than commencing one. He coughed and hesitated over his last sentence, forbore to meet the disturbingly experienced eyes concentrated on him, sought refuge in a platitude that camouflaged ugly but distant realities.

' ... And I'm quite sure, gentlemen, we're going to put up a really good show this time.'

He sat down.

The brigade-major rose to explain the details of the relief-model. The battalion officers crowded up to the table.

★ ★ ★

The grey dawn had already broken, revealing a landscape beyond imagining in its utter desolation. Its few trees had been splintered to short jagged points and the whole of it might have been stamped on by brutal giants. From unseen origins, a violence of rolling, throbbing thunder, of ear-splitting crashes, of rending disruptions repeated in savage little groups, interwove itself with the whining, wailing, cascade-like rush of projectiles in the air, ceaselessly renewed. Founts of black smoke, of flying mud and debris, leaped by thousands from the tortured earth. From under the low rain-swollen clouds, handfuls of dark smoke-puffs sprang from nothingness with quick sharp cracks and a prolonged menacing drone. On all the battle-field not a human figure was to be

---

[7] **orator:** good speech-maker

seen. It wanted ten minutes of zero-hour. The preliminary bombardment – swelled by partial counter-bombardment – was at its height.

Behind a wrecked trench parapet, an infantry subaltern, faceless and grotesque in a gas-mask, crouched with his eyes upon the dial of his wrist-watch. In the semi-fluid mud of the depression between one crumbled traverse and another, crouched some of his platoon, similarly anonymous and grotesque in their masks – weird figures divorced from humanity in a demoniac world divorced from normality. Each had a hand upon the weapon of his job – bayonet-tipped rifle, the divided paraphernalia of Lewis guns, bags of bombs. Among them, rolled on to his face, was the body of a man half-covered with a remnant of sack. The mud under him was red, and very fluid. A shell had landed in the trench just before. Two other men had completely vanished in its flash and smoke and stunning detonation. Nevertheless the others crouched patiently in the slush, their only horizon that broken trench parapet beyond which the noise of their own bombardment of the enemy position was one vast paralysing roar – the men they were about to kill, or by whom they would be killed, quite invisible to them.

The subaltern wondered what they were feeling. His own heart was thudding violently. His chest was gripped in a curiously stifling constriction; there was an emptiness in his abdomen, an internal sinking of his viscera that seemed to deprive him of physical strength. Their stolidity was odd, fantastic. In half an hour, how many of them would be alive? He himself? He shut off the thought, reverted to remembrance of his objective, repeated it doggedly to himself. 'N 25 c,' 'N 25 c.' It was the map reference to an infinitesimal section of the enemy second line. He was to press on to it, hang on, consolidate, wait for the second wave of the attack to pass over him, proceed 'mopping-up' behind that second wave. He visualised that objective as he had seen it in miniature on the relief-model, prayed inwardly that he would recognise it. The chances of it not being blasted out of original semblance by that pulverising rain of shells were remote. 'N 25 c' – he must get there, hang on. At all costs.

He looked again to his watch. Six minutes. Quite a time yet. Curse these gas-masks! One could not breathe in them. The nose-clip already hurt him. He shivered with a cold that soaked into his bones. That was a nice comfortable billet, that last one. Pretty girl, too. Duck your head! – *down!* CRASH! Fragments all gone over? – Yes. Sickening sound, that hissing rush as it arrives. Brutes! We must be giving 'em hell, though. Wonder how many of their machine-guns are escaping? Don't think – no use wondering. Know presently. Five minutes. Still five minutes. He had a sudden vision of that nice clean staff officer at the Brigade Conference in the barn, heard his diffident cultured voice – 'You will advance from here to there, and thence to somewhere else.' Easy enough for him! He was sitting now, cool and neat in a quiet office somewhere far back, waiting for reports, a cigarette in his mouth. (If only one could smoke in a gas-mask!) He wondered if the war would come to a sudden end if all the staffs who ordered attacks had personally to participate in them. The ironic imagination of it gave him a grim amusement. Four minutes. He willed his heart to beat normally, refused to let himself wonder what death was really like. (By Jove! That was a near one! Anyone hit? No. Good! *Damn* these shells!) Staff officers – yes – supposing they had to attack, too – they wouldn't be so glib then with their 'at all costs' – or would they? Good chaps, really, no doubt. Brave as anyone else, probably. Part of a system, that's all. Doing their jobs – ordering other people to wounds and death. Nice job. Wish he hadn't been such an enthusiastic ass. His father could have wangled it – nothing refused to really big contractors. His father – he'd be still in bed now, asleep – snoring – his mother – he saw his mother lying awake in the dawn – stop it, you ruddy fool! Three minutes. How the hand crawled! Was his watch stopping? Couldn't be – wound it when he synchronised last night. He would not think of anything – keep his brain a blank – blank – blank. Politicians at home, sleeping also in nice white beds, getting up to shout 'Win the war at all costs.'

Shut up – *shut – up!* Don't think. An eternity. Could one keep one's mind from thinking? God, this noise! Could understand chaps going mad. Two minutes. Only two minutes now. What's that? Three fellows blown up – best sergeant, too. Keep down, you idiots! One minute? It couldn't be really only one minute! It was. Less than one minute. He rose automatically, still crouching, eyes on that watch. Half a minute. A fraction – *Now!* He sprang for the parapet, waved his arm to the figures jerking up out of the trench. To right and left of him, hordes of other faceless figures had emerged as by magic, were all going one way.

What followed was a dream – a phantasmagoria[8] that had no reality. Those faceless men who dropped around him were not killed – or were phantoms who had never lived. The little group of tanks that lurched and plunged like ships in a rough sea were prehistoric creatures of a nightmare. The earth leaped up, almost at his feet, in quick red flash, black smoke and stunning concussion – leaped up all around him, in front, behind, on either side. The enemy counter-barrage. He wasn't killed. A vaguely apprehended miracle. Worst of it was these damned shell-holes – couldn't hurry – up to his waist in water that time – nice job for his servant cleaning off the mud. What was that insistent hissing, like an engine letting off steam, audible through the infernal din? Must get on – at all costs – N 25 c. Look at all those fellows throwing themselves down, taking cover! They weren't going to move. Kick 'em forward? Silly ass! Casualties. Hissing was machine-gun bullets. Marvel he wasn't hit. Charmed life. Thank God, enemy wire blown to bits. Enemy trench just beyond – hell erupting in it – no one visible. Anyone following? Yes. Scattered figures emerging through the smoke. Good chaps. He waved to them.

---

[8] *a phantasmagoria:* dream-like pictures

In their trenches. Ghastly mess. What a lot of blood a man has – never believe it – running down in a stream like that. That faceless snouted figure who had popped up from a hole. His revolver had gone off automatically at it. Figure had dropped. Wonderful how quick it was – fellow was alive then, dead now. What's that coming over? Bombs! Down in the mud – face down – can't help what it is. Damned latrine.[9] Ugh! *Bang-bang-bang!* Close call, that! Bombers! Bombers this way! Here they come – round the traverse – throw – dodge back – *bang-bang-bang-bang!* All quiet behind there? Yes. Only groans. Get on! Come on, all of you – don't matter what regiment you are – *come on!* Damn these gas-masks! Can't shout in 'em! Necessary, though. See that fellow whose mask had been perforated? Pretty ghastly, getting killed like that – just one gasp of air – poison. Place must be saturated with it. Ours or theirs? Ours first; theirs now. Half these shells gas-shells. Muffled bursts. Plenty of HE,[10] all the same. Shrapnel like rain. Enemy gunners enjoying themselves. My God! Down! Down quick! Damned machine-gun nest! How many hit? The whole bunch? No. Four. Keep down. Into the mud. Tanks! – where in Heaven's name are the tanks? That's what they're for. Here comes one. Wonderful things. It's seen the nest – slewed round – shouldn't like it coming for me. Uncanny great brute. There it goes – clatter of its track like an agricultural machine – letting 'em have it all round with all its guns – what's it like in there – copped up? There she goes. Over that damned nest like an ant-heap. Up we get! Cone on, lads! On! They can't hear in this infernal row. Can't shout properly either. *On!* That's right. Along here. Bombers first. Bombers and bayonet-men.

Further on. An aeroplane nose-diving – all but at the earth – in flames. Is this it? Must be second-line. Nothing looks like anything. All right for those fellows sitting behind with their nice neat maps and models. N 25 c – junction of trench with switch. That must be it, over

---

[9] **latrine:** lavatory
[10] **HE:** high explosive

there. Where that dead tank is – looks very dead, head foremost and still, great wound in its back. Smoke issuing from it. What happened to the crew? Not your business. Come on, boys! How many of 'em? Six – eight – nine. Is that all? Yes. No more. Must barricade the junction, quick. Where's the rest of the attack? Can't see anything in this smoke. There's some of 'em. Digging in. Barricade – barricade – anything – yes – dead men – better than nothing – they don't know – shove 'em along – that one, too. Push that arm down out of the way. No. He's dead all right. Thought he wasn't. Not the time to be squeamish ...

An eternity. All sorts of things had happened. Things he could not remember. But the shelling had never stopped. The enemy's shelling – and then their own, when the counter-attacks had developed – little groups of snout-faced men emerging suddenly from the mud, machine-gunning, throwing bombs, stabbing with bayonets when they got the chance – there had been incidents like individual murders. It was incredible that he was still alive. He still had men around him – anonymous in their gas-masks – but they were not the same men. These had adhered to him, he could not remember when or how. They crouched now in the mud of the shell-crater along with him. Together they had been driven back – had fought forward again in some sort of new attack that had caught them up and melted away – that was the time those snout-faced fellows had been trapped in a corner of a blocked trench – had been butchered redly, sickeningly – their bare hands trying to push away the bayonets. He remembered he had glanced at his watch. That must have been soon after one-thirty. A long time ago. Eternity. Was it the same day? There had been no victorious second wave behind which to 'proceed'. Some low-flying aeroplanes had circled over – suddenly appearing through the drenching rain that had lashed them for hours – had dropped boxes of ammunition that fell with a heavy splash on the liquid mud – most of them out of reach. The shelling was vindictive in its persistence. He could only hang on – hang on.

A counter-attack had sprung up from nowhere, been blotted out – mysteriously, from that apparently untenanted earth. There was a temporary lull. He was desperately hungry – his stomach gnawing at him – fevered with a maddening thirst. There was an 'iron-ration' in his haversack; he still had his water bottle. But he could neither eat nor drink in his gas-mask. It was death to remove it. Two men had died like that before he could stop them. The air was thick with gas, the ground splashed with chemical compound. The leaden sky was still raining in torrents. Little streams of yellow fluid ran down from the mud, mingled with water that was red. Mustard stuff. He was burned with it – it ate into them like corrosive acid – he had been careful, but it had come through his boots. He could not walk – none of those five recently-acquired men with him could walk. But they could still work the machine-gun whose tripod sank into the mud of the crater, brass-studded belt running through the breech – would use it, if, in the failing light, there were another counter-attack. That was improbable. Enemy wouldn't use mustard stuff if he meant to come back. But their job was to hang on. They were hanging on – hanging on, masked, soaked to the skin, like those other wretched little groups here and there whose presence he could divine rather than see. He had heard them 'loosing-off' a few minutes back, through that demoniac persistence of eternally-leaping shell-bursts whose red cores became ever more lurid in the gathering dusk.

It was black night – would have been black night if the opposing horizons had not flamed and flared incessantly from end to end. The thunder of massed guns, scarcely diminishing all day, had leaped to a new and frantic pitch of vehemence.[11] The mile-wide belt of churned mud where their shells fell was an inferno of blinding flashes, of shattering detonations. Both artilleries were 'taking it out of little brother' – each viciously destructive on the other's 'little brother', the infantry scattered sparsely in

---

[11] **vehemence:** intensity

a myriad shell-holes, denying to them further attack or counter-attack. Presently, the staffs behind would issue a communiqué, stating that the new front was 'stabilised'. He thought this as he lay on his back, head below his boots, in another shell-hole. He did not know how he came to be there. He remembered only the vivid red flash of an explosion in among them. There had been, oddly, no sound to it. When he had opened his eyes again the sky over his head had got quite dark, and he was in this position. He had found that he had no strength to alter it. He believed he had slept – once or twice. Thank God, anyway, the cries of that wounded wretch – out of sight somewhere – had ceased. The man had screamed that he was sinking into the mud. Suffocated? Very likely. He could not bother about it. Wounded himself, of course. Must be – or he would be able to change his position. God! how that mustard stuff burned! When would they pick up the wounded? Not till this shelling died down. Madness to try it now, of course. Sheer madness ... It was all madness ... a riot of madness ... . Must remember to keep this mask on.

He was in that barn, with the peaceful summer sunshine hot outside. That staff officer was speaking. 'We have done our best to make it easy for you – co-operation perfect – push on – at all costs – never mind your losses – attrition[12] – we can afford to lose men – he can't – millions more at home – millions – millions – millions – they'll all go forward into hell and die as we order 'em – we know what we're doing – we run the war, you see – it's *our* war – *our* war – good old war!' He half-woke from the delirium. Had the staff officer said that, really? He could not remember. Something like that. Poor b— infantry! The voice came again, over the heads of the crowd of infantry officers, grains of chaff dancing in the broad band of sunlight from the barn doors, a diffident, gentlemanly voice. 'I'm quite sure, gentlemen, we're going to put up a really good show this time.' My God, what a burst of shelling! Surely they couldn't

---

[12] **attrition:** fighting to wear down the enemy

be so mad as to attack again? All very well for them – *they* didn't attack – *they* ordered it – and then went to bye-bye in nice clean sheets. For God's sake, stop this infernal shelling! Each crash came inside his head. He would go mad with it. Mad. He was at home, lying in his own bed, his mother bending over him – he was ill, of course – home from school. Dreadful headache. Tortured with thirst – tortured. Why couldn't he drink? There was something over his face, preventing him – was it a cat, a cat lying over his mouth? Something like that had happened – once – beyond remembrance – a baby horror that revived in him in an automatic swift paroxysm.[13] He wrenched at it – wrenched off his gas-mask – had a last stare at lightning-lit sky as he choked ...

Back at Divisional Headquarters that day – in one of a neat row of semi-circular corrugated-iron Nissen huts, with gravel paths and flower-beds picked out with whitewashed stones in front of them – the Divisional Commander stood frowning by a staff officer who sat with a telephone to this ear.

The staff officer answered into the instrument. His tone was aggrieved.

'My dear fellow, it's no use cursing us. We're doing our best. Better get on to the Heavy Group. They brought their barrage right back on to our men – spoiled the show. What? Well, that's the reports I get – .' He changed his tone suddenly to one of profound respect. 'Yes, sir. Speaking, sir. Very good, sir. Yes, sir – we'll order it at once, sir. What time, sir? Half an hour, sir? You're arranging with the gunners? Very good. Good-bye, sir.' He put back the receiver, looked up to his superior. 'That's Corps strafing, sir – General himself – very angry we haven't gone further ahead – says we've left the flank of the 101st in the air. Wants another attack immediately – in half an hour.'

---

[13] **paroxysm:** sudden attack

The Divisional General tugged at his ragged white moustache.

'All very well for them!' he growled, in exasperation. 'These fellows behind never seem to realise what we're up against. What's the latest?'

The staff officer rose from his chair, went towards the wall where a large map, stuck with coloured pins was hanging. The Divisional General followed him with a heavy tread, beat his cane irritably against his brilliantly polished brown leggings.

'We've got some odd men hanging out here and here and here, sir,' he indicated the spots on the map – 'in the enemy second line – about all that's left of that brigade – the brigade on their right seems to have got completely smashed up by the enemy barrage and their confounded machine-guns – what's left of 'em are with what's left of the third brigade. We can send 'em forward again, sir, of course,' he concluded hopefully, with a glance at the Divisional Commander.

The Divisional Commander grunted. He listened for a moment to the unceasing thunder of the guns. The hut vibrated with their concussions.

'We must. Tell the brigades. They've got to get on at all costs.' He glanced at his subordinate. 'We're going to get unstuck for this, you and I, my friend – if they don't.' He sighed, staring at the map. A terrible number of Generals had 'come unstuck' lately. He pulled himself together, grinned sardonically at his subordinate. 'That'll mean the PBI again for *you*, my lad – and some damned training depôt for me. But not yet! Not without a fight for it. Is Corps warning the Heavies?'[14]

'Yes, sir.'

'Right. Get on to 'em yourself. And get on to the brigades. And for God's sake, see they co-ordinate this time.' He looked at his watch. 'Half an hour. One-thirty. Objectives as before. – And they've *got* to reach and hold the third line. *Got to* – mind! No excuses.'

The staff officer sat down, picked up the telephone again. It wasn't

---

[14] **Heavies:** large guns

their fault if the Division hadn't got on. They had done all they could. He almost began to hate this war. He rattled viciously at the instrument. Weren't they ever going to put him through? Lunch-time, too. The General was watching him. Should he 'straf'[15] – or be encouraging? 'Hallo – brigade! –'

Far away, in black night, on a ridge that was a morass underfoot, through an atmosphere that was poisoned, under vindictive murderous outbursts of shell-fire, soaked and weary infantrymen stumbled their difficult and dangerous ways to the line of water-filled shell-holes whence they would attack at the morrow's dawn. In a staff officer's room, twenty miles in rear of them, half a dozen uniformed press correspondents were writing despatches to a model thoughtfully supplied by higher authority. They were happy men, busy in a cloud of tobacco-smoke. One of them had just had a 'brain-wave', copied by the rest with artistic variations – 'The troops go forward with the joyous zest of men engaged in a great game – some units went into the last action dribbling a football ... It is only the skill and devotion of the Staff that makes scientific modern warfare possible on this vast scale. Even now, perhaps, the great public at home does not fully realise what war means. It has not come home to them as it does to us here –'

---

[15] **straf:** attack angrily

Activities

Close study (short story: narrative text)

I   Reread the first section of the story (pages 79–82). Does the battle attack seem well planned? Which details suggest that? What impressions do we get of the red-tabbed senior officers?

2   A sudden transition takes us to the battlefield. What impression do you get of the battlescape?

3   We enter the mind of a young officer and follow the attack. Which details of the fighting are most horrific? What does the officer think about:
   • the staff officers
   • his parents
   • politicians?

4   How exactly does he die?

5   The third section refers to staff officers at battle headquarters. Why has the attack failed? How do they react to the failure? What are they most worried about? What do they intend to do next?

Language study

6   Read 'Attack' by Siegfried Sassoon (1886–1967), which also describes a 1917 offensive. Then compare the ideas and language of the story and the poem. Which do you find more memorable?

Attack

At dawn the ridge emerges massed and dun
In the wild purple of the glow'ring sun,
Smouldering through spouts of drifting smoke that shroud
The menacing scarred slope; and, one by one,
Tanks creep and topple forward to the wire.
The barrage roars and lifts. Then, clumsily bowed
With bombs and guns and shovels and battle-gear,
Men jostle and climb to meet the bristling fire,
Lines of grey, muttering faces, masked with fear,
They leave their trenches, going over the top,
While time ticks blank and busy on their wrists,
And hope, with furtive eyes and grappling fists,
Flounders in mud. O Jesus, make it stop!

Reading

7   You might like to read *Some Desperate Glory*, the 1917 Ypres Battle diary of Edwin Campion Vaughan.

Ambulance Train

Helen Zenna Smith from Not So Quiet ... Stepdaughters of War (1930)

Helen Zenna Smith was the pen name of Evadne Price (1896–1985). Once an actress, she turned to journalism and writing children's books in the 1920s.

In 1929, a publisher asked her to create a comic imitation of the best-selling, German anti-war novel All Quiet on the Western Front *(1928) by Erich Remarque. She offered instead her own serious war story, based on the work of VAD (Voluntary Aid Detachment) women ambulance drivers in France. In the diary of a former VAD, who did not wish to publish, Price found powerful facts and memories to give force to her fiction and adopted a pen name to protect her source.* Not So Quiet ... Stepdaughters of War *caused enormous interest when it appeared first in parts in* The People *newspaper. Published in 1930, it won a French literary prize as the novel 'most calculated to promote international peace'.*

During the Second World War, Price became a war correspondent for The People *and was the first woman reporter to enter Belsen concentration camp in 1945. She subsequently reported the Nuremberg trials of leading Nazis.*

Not So Quiet *is fiercely written. It describes the experiences of a group of women ambulance drivers: 'Smithy' and her oddly nicknamed friends 'Tosh', 'Skinny', 'Etta Potato', 'The BF' and 'The Bug'. Coming from comfortable backgrounds, they have to get used to sleeplessness, rutted roads, lousiness, screaming stretcher cases, and the stench of gangrene. The book's particular targets are 'flag crazy civilians', like Smithy's mother and her rival in patriotic boasting, Mrs Evans-Mawnington. Smith is sickened by sentimental, armchair patriots who see her as 'one of England's splendid daughters, proud to do their bit for the dear old flag'. By contrast, she shows the hideous reality of her world:*

Trainloads of broken human-beings: half-mad men pleading to be put out of their misery; torn and bleeding and crazed men pitifully obeying orders like a herd of senseless cattle … smoke and bombs and lice and filth and noise, noise, noise … a world of cold sick fear, a dirty world of darkness and despair.

In this episode, Smith and her friends are waiting at night with their ambulances for the arrival of a train bringing casualties from the front.

Some of the girls begin to tramp about the station yard. I am too numb to get down. I suppose I still possess feet, though I cannot feel them. The wind has dropped slightly, but it seems to get colder and colder. Oh, this cold of France. I have never experienced anything remotely resembling it. It works through one's clothing, into one's flesh and bones. It is not satisfied till it is firmly ingrained in one's internal regions, from whence it never really moves.

It has been freezing hard for over a week now. The bare trees in the road are loaded with icicles, … tall trees, ugly and gaunt and gallows-like till the whiteness veiled them – transforming them into objects of weird beauty.

Etta Potato and The Bug want me to come down. They are having a walking race with Tosh for cigarettes – the winner to collect one each from the losers. Won't I join in? I refuse, … I am too numb to move. Off they start across the snow-covered yard. Tosh wins easily. Their laughter rings out as she extorts her winnings there and then. All of a sudden their laughter ceases. They fly back to their posts. The convoy must be sighted. I crane my neck. Yes. The stretcher-bearers stop smoking and line up along the platform. Ambulance doors are opened in readiness. All is bustle. Everyone on the alert. Cogs in the great machinery. I can hear the noise of the train distinctly now, … sound travels a long way in the snow in these death-still early morning hours before the dawn. Louder and louder.

If the War goes on and on and on and I stay out here for the duration,

I shall never be able to meet a train-load of casualties without the same ghastly nausea[1] stealing over me as on that first never-to-be-forgotten night. Most of the drivers grow hardened after the first week. They fortify themselves with thoughts of how they are helping to alleviate the sufferings of wretched men, and find consolation in so thinking. But I cannot. I am not the type that breeds warriors. I am the type that should have stayed at home, that shrinks from blood and filth, and is completely devoid of pluck.[2] In other words, I am a coward … A rank coward. I have no guts. It takes every ounce of will-power I possess to stick to my post when I see the train rounding the bend. I choke my sickness back into my throat, and grip the wheel, and tell myself it is all a horrible nightmare … soon I shall awaken in my satin-covered bed on Wimbledon Common … what I can picture with such awful vividness doesn't really exist.

I have schooled myself to stop fainting at the sight of blood. I have schooled myself not to vomit at the smell of wounds and stale blood, but view these sad bodies with professional calm I shall never be able to. I may be helping to alleviate the sufferings of wretched men, but commonsense rises up and insists that the necessity should never have arisen. I become savage at the futility. A war to end war, my mother writes. Never. In twenty years it will repeat itself. And twenty years after that. Again and again, as long as we breed women like my mother and Mrs Evans-Mawnington. And we are breeding them. Etta Potato and The BF – two out of a roomful of six. Mother and Mrs Evans-Mawnington all over again.

Oh, come with me, Mother and Mrs Evans-Mawnington. Let me show you the exhibits straight from the battlefield. This will be something original to tell your committees, while they knit their endless miles of khaki scarves, … something to spout from the platform at your recruiting meetings. Come with me. Stand just there.

Here we have the convoy gliding into the station now, slowly, so

---

[1] **nausea:** sickness
[2] **pluck:** courage

slowly. In a minute it will disgorge its sorry cargo. My ambulance doors are open, waiting to receive. See, the train has stopped. Through the occasionally drawn blinds you will observe the trays slotted into the sides of the train. Look closely, Mother and Mrs, Evans-Mawnington, and you shall see what you shall see. Those trays each contain something that was once a whole man ... the heroes who have done their bit for King and country ... the heroes who marched blithely through the streets of London Town singing 'Tipperary',[3] while you cheered and waved your flags hysterically. They are not singing now, you will observe. Shut your ears, Mother and Mrs Evans-Mawnington, lest their groans and heart-rending cries linger as long in your memory as in the memory of the daughter you sent out to help win the War.

See the stretcher-bearers lifting the trays one by one, slotting them deftly into my ambulance. Out of the way quickly, Mother and Mrs Evans-Mawnington – lift your silken skirts aside ... a man is spewing blood, the moving has upset him, finished him ... He will die on the way to hospital if he doesn't die before the ambulance is loaded. I know ... all this is old history to me. Sorry this has happened. It isn't pretty to see a hero spewing up his life's blood in public, is it? Much more romantic to see him in the picture papers being awarded the VC, even if he is minus a limb or two. A most unfortunate occurrence!

That man strapped down? That raving, blaspheming creature scream-ing filthy words you don't know the meaning of ... words your daughter uses in everyday conversation, a habit she has contracted from vulgar contact of this kind. Oh, merely gone mad, Mother and Mrs Evans-Mawnington. He may have seen a headless body running on and on, with blood spurting from the trunk. The crackle of the frost-stiff dead men packing the duck-boards watertight may have gradually undermined his reason. There are many things the sitters tell me on our long night rides that could have done this.

---

[3] **'Tipperary':** a soldiers' song

No, not shell-shock. The shell-shock cases take it more quietly as a rule, unless they are suddenly startled. Let me find you an example. Ah, the man they are bringing out now. The one staring straight ahead at nothing ... twitching, twitching, twitching, each limb working in a different direction, like a Jumping Jack worked by a jerking string. Look at him, both of you. Bloody awful, isn't it, Mother and Mrs Evans-Mawnington? That's shell-shock. If you dropped your handbag on the platform, he would start to rave as madly as the other. What? You won't try the experiment? You can't watch him? Why not? *Why not?* I have to, every night. Why the hell can't you do it for once? Damn your eyes.

Forgive me, Mother and Mrs Evans-Mawnington. That was not the kind of language a nicely-brought-up young lady from Wimbledon Common uses. I forget myself. We will begin again.

See the man they are fitting into the bottom slot. He is coughing badly. No, not pneumonia. Not tuberculosis. Nothing so picturesque. Gently, gently, stretcher-bearers ... he is about done. He is coughing up clots of pinky-green filth. Only his lungs, Mother and Mrs Evans-Mawnington. He is coughing well to-night. That is gas. You've heard of gas, haven't you? It burns and shrivels the lungs to ... to the mess you see on the ambulance floor there. He's about the age of Bertie, Mother. Not unlike Bertie, either, with his gentle brown eyes and fair curly hair. Bertie would look up pleadingly like that in between coughing up his lungs ... The son you have so generously given to the War. The son you are so eager to send out to the trenches before Roy Evans-Mawnington, in case Mrs Evans-Mawnington scores over you at the next recruiting meeting ... 'I have given my only son.'

Cough, cough, little fair-haired boy. Perhaps somewhere your mother is thinking of you ... boasting of the life she has so nobly given ... the life you thought was your own, but which is hers to squander as she thinks fit. 'My boy is not a slacker,[4] thank God.' Cough away, little boy, cough

---

[4] *slacker:* someone who avoids war service

away. What does it matter, providing your mother doesn't have to face the shame of her son's cowardice?

These are sitters. The man they are hoisting up beside me, and the two who sit in the ambulance. Blighty cases ... broken arms and trench feet ... mere trifles. The smell? Disgusting, isn't it? Sweaty socks and feet swollen to twice their size ... purple, blue, red ... big black blisters filled with yellow matter. Quite a colour-scheme, isn't it? Have I made you vomit? I must again ask pardon. My conversation is daily growing less refined. Spew and vomit and sweat ... I had forgotten these words are not used in the best drawing-rooms of Wimbledon Common.

But I am wasting time. I must go in a minute. I am nearly loaded. The stretcher they are putting on one side? Oh, a most ordinary exhibit, ... the groaning man to whom the smallest jolt is a red hell ... a mere belly-ful of shrapnel. They are holding him over till the next journey. He is not as urgent as the helpless thing there, that trunk without arms and legs, the remnants of a human being, incapable even of pleading to be put out of his misery because his jaw has been half shot away ... No, don't meet his eyes, they are too alive. Something of their malevolence might remain with you all the rest of your days, ... those sock-filled, committee-crowded days of yours.

Gaze on the heroes who have so nobly upheld your traditions, Mother and Mrs Evans-Mawnington. Take a good look at them ... The heroes you will sentimentalise over until peace is declared, and allow to starve for ever and ever, amen, afterwards. Don't go. Spare a glance for my last stretcher, ... that gibbering, unbelievable, unbandaged thing, a wagging lump of raw flesh on a neck, that was a face a short time ago, Mother and Mrs Evans-Mawnington. Now it might be anything ... a lump of liver, raw bleeding liver, that's what it resembles more than anything else, doesn't it? We can't tell its age, but the whimpering moan sounds young, somehow. Like the fretful whimpers of a sick little child ... a tortured little child ... puzzled whimpers. Who is he? For all you know, Mrs Evans-Mawnington, he is your Roy. He might be anyone at all, so why not your Roy? One shapeless lump of raw liver is like another shapeless lump of raw liver. What do you say? Why don't they cover him up with bandages? How the hell do I know? I have often wondered myself, ... but they don't. Why do you turn away? That's only liquid fire.[5] You've heard of liquid fire? Oh, yes. I remember your letter ... *'I hear we've started to use liquid fire, too. That will teach those Germans. I hope we use lots and lots of it.'* Yes, you wrote that. You were glad some new fiendish torture had been invented by the chemists who are running this war. You were delighted to think some German mother's son was going to have the skin stripped from his poor face by liquid fire ... Just as some equally patriotic German mother rejoiced when she first heard the sons of Englishwomen were to be burnt and tortured by the very newest war gadget out of the laboratory.

Don't go, Mother and Mrs Evans-Mawnington, ... don't go. I am loaded, but there are over thirty ambulances not filled up. Walk down the line. Don't go, unless you want me to excuse you while you retch your insides out as I so often do. There are stretchers and stretchers you haven't seen yet ... Men with hopeless dying eyes who don't want to die ... men with hopeless living eyes who don't want to live. Wait, wait, I have so much, so much to show you before you return to your committees and your recruiting meetings, before you add to your bag of recruits ... those young recruits you enroll so proudly with your patriotic speeches, your red, white and blue rosettes, your white feathers,[6] your insults, your lies ... any bloody lie to secure a fresh victim.

What? You cannot stick it any longer? You are going? I didn't think you'd stay. But I've got to stay, haven't I? ... I've got to stay. You've got me out here, and you'll keep me out here. You've got me haloed. I am one of the Splendid Young Women who are winning the war ...

'Loaded. Six stretchers and three sitters!'

---

[5] **liquid fire:** a flame-thrower, a weapon that ejects a stream or spray of liquid fire
[6] **white feathers:** given to 'cowards', men not in uniform

I am away. I slow up at the station gate. The sergeant is waiting with his pencil and list.

I repeat, 'Six stretchers and three sitters.'

'Number Eight.'

He ticks off my ambulance. I pass out of the yard.

Activities

Close study (fiction based on diary: narrative text)

1 'Smithy' sits in her ambulance in the middle of the night. What does she feel and see as she waits for the ambulance train? How does she see herself?
2 What impressions do you get of Mother's and Mrs Evans-Mawnington's lives at home? What are their attitudes to the war?
3 Read again the descriptions of the war victims that 'Smithy' helps from the train. Which details shock you about each one? Which was the worst?
4 What is Smith's intention in writing this episode?

Language study

5 This piece is written with its verbs in the present tense. Why is this effective?
6 To add force to her thoughts, 'Smithy' uses many colloquialisms (words and phrases from everyday speech). Find twenty examples. What effect do they have on the reader?

Writing

7 Compare the ideas and writing method of this passage with perhaps the most famous of all war poems, 'Dulce et Decorum Est' by Wilfred Owen. Which do you feel is the more powerful, prose or poem?
8 Write a short letter from Mother to 'Smithy', outlining her war work, and her vision of the war and her daughter's part in it. (Mention her rival, Mrs Evans-Mawnington!)

Reading

9 Other excellent descriptions of women's activity in the 1914–18 war that you might like to read include *Testament of Youth* by Vera Brittain and *Diary Without Dates* by Enid Bagnold.

Second World War (1939–1945)

When Nazi Germany attacked Poland in September 1939, years of appeasement of Hitler ended as Britain and France declared war. The German 'Blitzkrieg' (lightning war) in 1940 left them in control of much of western Europe, including France. The Battle of Britain in summer 1940 kept Britain free. The war expanded when Germany attacked the Soviet Union in June 1941, and when the Japanese struck at the American naval base at Pearl Harbor in Hawaii in December.

The war became world-wide, fought in massive air campaigns over Germany; in the North African desert; in the snows of the Soviet Union; from island to island in the Pacific. It was a war of huge human drama: the British escape from Dunkirk in 1940; the British victory over the Germans at El Alamein in 1942; the Soviet defeat of a whole German army at Stalingrad in 1942–3; the Allied D-Day invasion of Normandy in June 1944. Memories of the war are now haunted by two immense horrors: the 'Holocaust' or mass killing of Jewish people and other minorities in Nazi-occupied Europe, and the explosions, that ended the war, of two American atomic bombs at Hiroshima and Nagasaki in Japan in August 1945.

Resources for pages 103–163

Books *The Second World War* by Martin Gilbert
Videos *The World at War* by ITV
They Were Victorious by Cromwell Productions (four videos)
Websites www.bbc.co.uk/history/wwtwo
www.iwm.org.uk

The Finest Hour: Britain at War 1940

The year 1940, described by Winston Churchill, the wartime Prime Minister, as Britain's 'finest hour', was a year of astonishing drama. In May, the German 'Blitzkrieg' (lightning war) attack on France forced the British Army to retreat to Dunkirk, where thousands of soldiers were, by a 'miracle', it seemed, evacuated to England.

The air Battle of Britain raged over the southern counties from July to October, 1940. It reached its heights in what the writer H.E. Bates called the 'torturingly beautiful' September: 'Those who lived in the south east that summer will never forget the irony of its ethereal beauty and its deathly, deathless conflict'. The Royal Air Force lost 915 aircraft but the British 'Spitfire' and 'Hurricane' fighters shot down 1,733 German machines. The Nazis could not destroy British air power and their projected invasion of Britain was abandoned.

The youth, daring and courage of the RAF pilots have become legendary. Many died horribly, trapped in burning aircraft. On 20 August, Churchill praised them: 'Never in the field of human conflict was so much owed by so many to so few'.

Battle of Britain Pilot

John Beard from *Their Finest Hour* (1941)

John Beard, a 21-year-old 'Hurricane' pilot, one of 'The Few', described a September air battle over London. The article, in a book aimed at the American market, appeared in 1941, so certain technical details were censored by the government.

★

I was supposed to be away on a day's leave but dropped back to the aero-drome to see if there was a letter from my wife. When I found out that *all* the squadrons had gone off into action I decided to stand by, because obviously something big was happening. While I was climbing into my flying kit, our Hurricanes came slipping back out of the sky to refuel, reload ammunition, and take off again. The returning pilots were full of talk about flocks of enemy bombers and fighters which were trying to break through along the Thames Estuary. You couldn't miss hitting them, they said. Off to the East I could hear the steady roll of anti-aircraft fire. It was a brilliant afternoon with a flawless blue sky. I was crazy to be off.

An instant later an aircraftman rushed up with orders for me to make up a flight with some of the machines then reloading. My own Hurricane was a nice old kite,[1] though it had a habit of flying left wing low at the slightest provocation. But since it had already accounted for fourteen German aircraft before I inherited it, I thought it had some luck, and I was glad when I squeezed myself into the same old seat again and grabbed the 'stick'.

We took off in two flights,[2] and as we started to gain height over the station we were told over the RT[3] to keep circling for a while until we were made up to a stronger force. That didn't take long, and soon there was a complete squadron[4] including a couple of Spitfires which had wandered in from somewhere.

Then came the big thrilling moment: ACTION ORDERS. Distantly I heard the hum of the generator in my RT earphones and then the voice of the ground controller crackling through with the call signs: '[Censored].' Then the order: 'Fifty plus bombers, one hundred plus fighters over

---

[1] **kite:** aeroplane
[2] **two flights:** six fighters
[3] **RT:** radio telephone
[4] **complete squadron:** twelve machines

Canterbury at 15,000 heading north-east. Your vector[5] nine zero degrees. Over!'

We were flying in four V formations of three. I was flying No. 3 in Red flight, which was the squadron-leader's and thus the leading flight. On we went, wingtips to left and right slowly rising and falling, the roar of our twelve Merlins[6] drowning all other sound. We crossed over London which, at 20,000 feet seemed just a haze of smoke from its countless chimneys, with nothing visible except the faint glint of the barrage balloons and the wriggley silver line of the Thames.

I had too much to do watching the instruments and keeping formation to do much thinking. But once I caught a reflected glimpse of myself in the windscreen – a goggled, bloated, fat thing with the tube of my oxygen supply protruding gruesomely sideways from the mask which hid my mouth. Suddenly I was back at school again, on a hot afternoon when the Headmaster was taking the Sixth and droning on and on about the later Roman Emperors. The boy on my right was showing me surreptitiously some illustrations which he had pinched out of his father's medical books during the last holidays. I looked like one of those pictures.

It was an amazingly vivid memory as if school was only yesterday. And half my mind was thinking what wouldn't I then have given to be sitting in a Hurricane belting along at 350 miles an hour and out for a kill. *Me* defending London! I grinned at my old self at the thought.

Minutes went by. Green fields and roads were now beneath us. I scanned the sky and the horizon for the first glimpse of the Germans. A new vector came through on the RT and we swung round with the sun behind us. Swift on the heels of this I heard Yellow flight leader call through the earphones: '[Censored].' I looked quickly towards Yellow's position and there *they* were!

---

[5] **vector:** steering course to intercept
[6] **Merlins:** aircraft engines

It was really a terrific sight and quite beautiful. First they seemed just a cloud of light as the sun caught the many glistening chromium parts of their engines, their windshields and the spin of their airscrew discs. Then as our squadron hurtled nearer, the details stood out. I could see the bright-yellow noses of Messerschmitt fighters sandwiching the bombers, and could even pick out some of the types. The sky seemed full of them, packed in layers thousands of feet deep. They came on steadily, wavering up and down along the horizon. 'Oh, golly,' I thought, 'golly, golly ... '

And then any tension I had felt on the way suddenly left me. I was elated but very calm. I leaned over and switched on my reflector sight, flicked the catch on the guns button from 'Safe' to 'Fire', and lowered my seat till the circle and dot on the reflector sight shone darkly red in front of my eyes.

The squadron-leader's voice came through the earphones giving tactical orders. We swung round in a great circle to attack on their beam – into the thick of them. Then, on the order, down we went. I took my hand from the throttle lever so as to get both hands on the stick and my thumb played neatly across the gun button. You have to steady a fighter just as you have to steady a rifle before you fire it.

My Merlin screamed as I went down in a steeply-banked dive on to the tail of a forward line of Heinkels. I knew the air was full of aircraft flinging themselves about in all directions but, hunched and snuggled down behind my sight, I was conscious only of the Heinkel I had picked out. As the angle of my dive increased, the enemy machine loomed larger in the sight field, heaved towards the red dot, and then he was there!

I had an instant's flash of amazement at the Heinkel proceeding so regularly on its way with a fighter on its tail. 'Why doesn't the fool *move!*' I thought, and actually caught myself flexing my muscles into the action *I* would have taken had I been he.

When he was square across the sight I pressed the button. There was a smooth trembling of my Hurricane as the eight-gun squirt shot out. I gave him a two-second burst and then another. Cordite fumes blew back into the cockpit making an acrid mixture with the smell of hot oil and the air compressors.

I saw my first burst go in and just as I was on top of him and turning away I noticed a red glow inside the bomber. I turned tightly into position again and now saw several short tongues of flame lick out along the fuselage. Then he went down in a spin, blanketed with smoke and with pieces flying off.

I left him plummeting down and, horsing back on my stick, climbed up again for more. The sky was clearing but ahead towards London I saw a small tight formation of bombers completely encircled by a ring of Messerschmitts. They were still heading north. As I raced forward three flights of Spitfires came zooming up from beneath them in a sort of Prince of Wales feathers manoeuvre. They burst through upwards and outwards, their guns going all the time. They must have each got one for an instant later I saw the most extraordinary sight of eight German bombers and fighters diving earthward together in flames.

I turned away again and streaked after some distant specks ahead. Diving down, I noticed that the running progress of the battle had brought me over London again. I could see the network of streets with the green space of Kensington Gardens, and I had an instant's glimpse of the Round Pond where I sailed boats when I was a child. In that moment and as I was rapidly overhauling the Germans ahead, a Dornier 17 sped right across my line of flight closely pursued by a Hurricane. And behind the Hurricane came two Messerschmitts. He was too intent to have seen them and they had not seen me! They were coming slightly towards me. It was perfect. A kick at the rudder and I swung in towards them, thumbed the gun button and let them have it. The first burst was placed just the right distance ahead of the leading Messerschmitt. He ran slap into it and he simply came to pieces in the air. His companion, with one of the speediest and most brilliant 'get-outs' I have ever seen, went right away in a half Immelmann turn.[7] I missed him completely. He must almost have been hit by the pieces of the leader but he got away. I hand it to him.

At that moment some instinct made me glance up at my rear view mirror and spot two Messerschmitts closing in on my tail. Instantly I hauled back on the stick and streaked upwards. And just in time. For as I flicked into the climb I saw the tracer streaks pass beneath me. As I turned I had a quick look round the 'Office' [cockpit]. My fuel reserve was running out and I had only about a second's supply of ammunition left. I was certainly in no condition to take on two Messerschmitts. But they seemed no more eager than I was. Perhaps they were in the same position, for they turned away for home. I put my nose down and did likewise.

Only on the way back did I realise how hot I was. I had forgotten to adjust the ventilator apparatus in all the stress of fighting, and hadn't noticed the thermometer. With the sun on the windows all the time, the inside of the 'Office' was like an oven. Inside my flying suit I was in a bath of perspiration, and sweat was cascading down my face. I was dead tired and my neck ached constantly from turning my head on the look-out when going in and out of dog-fights. Over east the sky was flecked with AA[8] puffs, but I did not bother to investigate. Down I went, home.

At the station there was only time for a few minutes' stretch, a hurried report to the Intelligence Officer and a brief comparing of notes with the other pilots. So far my squadron seemed to be intact in spite of a terrific two hours in which we had accounted for at least thirty enemy aircraft.

But there was more to come. It was now about 4 pm, and I gulped down some tea while the ground crews checked my Hurricane. Then with about three flights collected we took off again. We seemed to be

---

[7] **Immelmann turn:** looping turn

[8] **AA:** anti-aicaft fire

rather longer this time circling and gaining height above the station before the orders came through on the RT. It was to patrol an area along the Thames Estuary at 20,000 feet. But we never got there.

We had no sooner got above the docks when we ran into the first lot of enemy bombers. They were coming up in a line about 5,000 feet below us. The line stretched on and on across the horizon. Above, on our level, were assorted groups of enemy fighters. Some were already in action with our fellows spinning and twirling among them. Again I got that tightening feeling at the throat, for it really was a sight to make you gasp.

But we all knew what to do. We went for the bombers. Kicking her over I went down after the first of them, a Heinkel I I I. He turned away as I approached chiefly because some of our fellows had already broken into the line and scattered it. Before I got up he had been joined by two more. They were forming a V and heading south across the river.

I went after them. Closing in on the tail of the left one I ran into a stream of cross-fire from all three. How it missed me I don't know. For a second the whole air in front was thick with tracer trails. It seemed to be coming straight at me only to curl away by the windows and go lazily past. I felt one slight bang however and, glancing quickly, saw a hole at the end of my starboard wing. Then, as the Heinkel drifted across my sights, I pressed the button – once ... twice ... Nothing happened.

I panicked for a moment till I looked down and saw that I had forgotten to turn the safety catch knob to the 'Fire' position. I flicked it over at once and in that instant saw that three bombers, to hasten their getaway, had jettisoned[9] all their bombs. They seemed to peel off in a steady stream. We were over the southern outskirts of London now and I remember hoping that most of them would miss the little houses and plunge into fields.

But dropping the bombs did not help my Heinkel. I let him have a

---

[9] **jettisoned:** dropped casually

long burst at close range which got him right in the 'office', I saw him turn slowly over and go down, and followed to give him another squirt. Just then there was a terrific crash in front of me. Something flew past my window, and the whole aircraft shook as the engine raced itself to pieces. I had been hit by AA fire aimed at the bombers, my airscrew had been blown off and I was going down in a spin.

The next few seconds were a bit wild and confused. I remember switching off and flinging back the sliding roof almost in one gesture. Then I tried to vault out through the roof. But I had forgotten to release my safety belt. As I fumbled at the pin the falling aircraft gave a twist which shot me through the open cover. Before I was free the airstream hit me like a solid blow and knocked me sideways. I felt my arm hit something, and then I was falling over and over with fields and streets and sky gyrating[10] madly past my eyes.

I grabbed at the rip-cord on my 'chute.[11] Missed it. Grabbed again. Missed it. That was no fun. Then I remember saying to myself, 'This won't do. Take it easy, take it slowly.' I tried again and found the rip-cord grip and pulled. There was a terrific wrench at my thighs and then I was floating still and peacefully with my 'brolly' canopy billowing above my head.

The rest was lovely. I sat at my ease just floating gradually down, breathing deep, and looking around. I was drifting across London again at about 2,000 feet. Just below me I spotted another parachute, a German, probably from the bomber I had shot down. I shouted to him but he did not appear to hear me. He was about 500 feet lower and falling faster than me.

I drifted toward the river. Lower now and over the crowded Dockland area I could plainly see the wreck of houses which bombers had left in their wake, and the smoke of fires. At one point I could actually see fire-engines hurtling along a street. There was no other traffic visible. The

---

[10] **gyrating:** turning
[11] **'chute:** parachute

northward fringe of London's houses came nearer. I could see that I had plenty of room to miss the crowded roofs and land in open fields.

I actually landed in an allotment garden, my trailing body and the parachute harness simply massacring whole rows of runner-beans. I brought up finally in a compost heap festooned with tendrils and the peas and beans I dragged with me.

I lay there for a minute or two, just glad to be alive. In that short while a whole posse of Home Guards and air raid wardens burst into the allotment and surrounded me. I think I was a little bit screwy because I just lay there and smiled at them, although they were looking so wary and ferocious. Nice ordinary little blokes. I could have kissed them.

Then I said, 'Help me out of this harness, will you?' I found I could not move my right arm which hurt a lot from that bump I felt as I had baled out. They obliged cheerfully, handling me as carefully as if I was made of glass. I started to say how sorry I was that I had made such a mess of the runner-beans when someone stuck a cigarette in my mouth.

They helped me to get my tunic off while I had a look at my arm. It wasn't bad. My shoulder was out a bit and that was all except for a few bruises on my leg. We walked in a procession to the allotment entrance where the chief warden said his car was waiting. By coincidence I had landed only three or four miles from my own station, and the warden offered to drive me there. But just as we got to the road an ambulance drove up. 'That's service for you,' said one of the wardens. So I had to climb in and be driven back to the station Medical Officer. I was minus my Hurricane, I had a slightly damaged shoulder, but I was plus two German bombers and a fighter. It was the end of a perfect day.

Activities

Close study (reportage: non-fiction recount text)

1 Beard is a skilful descriptive writer. Find some passages where he allows you to see and hear scenes around him as he flies.

2 Beard is very young. Where does he bring in boyhood memories to contrast with his present dangerous life?

3 What examples does he give of the discomforts and stresses of flying a 'Hurricane' in war?

4 He makes light of the dangers he faces. What are these?

5 How exactly is he shot down and how does he escape from his falling aircraft?

6 What impression of Beard's character do you get from this passage? What is his attitude to fighting in war?

Language study

7 How do the technical explanations and the 'censored' boxes add conviction to this drama of air war?

8 Beard writes in a very colloquial way, using a mixture of young man's and RAF slang. Find examples of this.

Writing

9 Compose a poem in three verses about the air battles over London:
  • one by a young pilot like Beard
  • one by a member of a German bomber crew
  • one by a civilian watching the fighting from the London streets.

Reading

10 You might like to read *The Last Enemy* by Richard Hillary, a classic memoir written by a 'Spitfire' pilot.

The London Blitz

Edward Murrow from *This is London* (1941)

On Saturday, 7 September 1940, 348 German bombers, in a twenty mile wide fleet, attacked London in the late afternoon. Four hundred and forty-eight people died. Fighters could shoot down the German raiders by day but there was little defence at night. After this first offensive, there were raids every day or night up to 2 November. First the East End docks and then the whole of central London became targets. 'A great fire was blazing,' remembered a raid survivor, 'and the whole street was piled several feet high with glass and rubble. In the sky the light from fires was brilliant. It looked like Blake's pictures of Hell.'

The raids reached a furious climax on 29 December when the City of London was set on fire. The dome of St Paul's Cathedral was silhouetted against flames and smoke. Some 20,000 people died in the London Blitz, 3000 of them in its final, and worst, night on 10 May, 1941.

Edward Murrow (1908–1965) was a very distinguished American journalist who worked for CBS, a major US radio network. Posted to London in 1939, he described the Battle of Britain and the Blitz to American listeners, each broadcast beginning dramatically: 'This (pause) is London.'

The USA remained neutral until 1941, but Murrow's clear, compelling word pictures won sympathy for Britain's lone stand against the German Nazis. A fellow journalist commented: 'Murrow made you feel about the possible defeat of Britain as personally as you would about the death of a child.'

September 8, 1940

Yesterday afternoon – it seems days ago now – I drove down to the East End of London, the East India Dock Road, Commercial Road, through

Silvertown, down to the mouth of the Thames Estuary. It was a quiet and almost pleasant trip through those streets running between rows of working-class houses, with the cranes, the docks, the ships, and the oil tanks off on the right. We crossed the River and drove up on a little plateau, which gave us a view from the mouth of the Thames to London. And then an air-raid siren,[1] called 'Weeping Willie' by the men who tend it, began its uneven screaming. Down on the coast the white puffballs of anti-aircraft fire began to appear against a steel-blue sky. The first flight of the German bombers was coming up the river to start the twelve-hour attack on London. They were high and not very numerous. The Hurricanes and Spitfires were already in the air, climbing for altitude above the nearby aerodrome. The fight moved inland and out of sight. Things were relatively quiet for about half an hour. Then the British fighters returned. And five minutes later the German bombers, flying in V-formation, began pouring in. The anti-aircraft fire was good. Sometimes it seemed to burst right on the nose of the leading machine, but still they came on. On the aerodrome, ground crews swarmed over those British fighters, fitting ammunition belts and pouring in petrol. As soon as one fighter was ready, it took the air, and there was no waiting for flight leaders or formation. The Germans were already coming back, down the river, heading for France.

Up toward London we could see billows of smoke fanning out above the river; and over our heads the British fighters, climbing almost straight up, trying to intercept the bombers before they got away. It went on for two hours and then the 'all clear'. We went down to a near-by pub for dinner. Children were already organising a hunt for bits of shrapnel.[2] Under some bushes beside the road there was a baker's cart. Two boys, still sobbing, were trying to get a quivering mare back between the shafts. The lady who ran the pub told us that these raids were bad for the chickens, the

---

[1] *siren:* warning signal
[2] *bits of shrapnel:* fragments of anti-aircraft shells

dogs and the horses. A toothless old man of nearly seventy came in and asked for a pint of mild and bitter, confided that he had always, all his life, gone to bed at eight o'clock and found now that three pints of beer made him drowsy-like so he could sleep through any air raid.

Before eight the siren sounded again. We went back to a haystack near the aerodrome. The fires up River had turned the moon blood red. The smoke had drifted down till it formed a canopy over the Thames; the guns were working all round us, the bursts looking like fireflies in a southern summer night. The Germans were sending in two or three planes at a time, sometimes only one, in relays. They would pass over-head. The guns and lights would follow them, and in about five minutes we could hear the hollow grunt of the bombs. Huge pear-shaped bursts of flame would rise up into the smoke and disappear. The world was upside down.

It was like a shuttle service, the way the German planes came up the Thames, the fires acting as a flare path. Often they were above the smoke. The searchlights bored into that black roof, but couldn't pene-trate it. They looked like long pillars supporting a black canopy. Suddenly all the lights dashed off and blackness fell right to the ground. It grew cold. We covered ourselves with hay. The shrapnel clicked as it hit the concrete road near by, and still the German bombers came.

This afternoon we drove back to the East End of London. It was like an obstacle race – two blocks to the right, then left for four blocks, then straight on for a few blocks, and right again ... streets roped off, houses and shops smashed ... a few dirty-faced, tow-headed children standing on a corner, holding their thumbs up, the sign of the men who came back from Dunkirk ... three red buses drawn up in a line waiting to take the homeless away ... men with white scarfs round their necks instead of collars and ties, leading dull-eyed, empty-faced women across to the buses. Most of them carried little cheap cardboard suit cases and some-times bulging paper shopping-bags. That was all they had left. There was still fire and smoke along the river, but the firefighters and the demolition squads[3] have done their work well.

September 21, 1940

I'm standing on a roof-top looking out over London. At the moment everything is quiet. For reasons of personal as well as national security, I'm unable to tell you the exact location from which I'm speaking. Off to my left, far away in the distance, I can see just that faint-red, angry snap of anti-aircraft bursts against the steel-blue sky, but the guns are so far away that it's impossible to hear them from this location. About five minutes ago the guns in the immediate vicinity[4] were working. I can look across at a building not far away and see something that looks like a flash of white paint down the side, and I know from daylight observation that about a quarter of that building had disappeared – hit by a bomb the other night. Streets fan out in all directions from here, and down on one street I can see a single red light and just faintly the outline of a sign standing in the middle of the street. And again I know what that sign says, because I saw it this afternoon. It says DANGER – UNEXPLODED BOMB. Off to my left still I can see just that red snap of the anti-aircraft fire.

I was up here earlier this afternoon and looking out over these house-tops, looking all the way to the dome of St Paul's. I saw many flags flying from staffs. No one ordered these people to put out the flag. They simply feel like flying the Union Jack above their roof. No one told them to do it, and no flag up there was white. I can see one or two of them just stirring very faintly in the breeze now. You may be able to hear the sound of guns off in the distance very faintly, like someone kicking a tub. Now they're silent. Four searchlights reach up, disappear in the light of a three-quarter moon. I should say at the moment there are probably three aircraft in the general vicinity of London, as one can tell by the movement of the lights

---

[3] **demolition squads:** men who destroyed buildings to prevent fires spreading

[4] **vicinity:** neighbourhood

and the flash of the anti-aircraft guns. But at the moment in the central area everything is quiet. More searchlights spring up over on my right. I think probably in a minute we shall have the sound of guns in the immediate vicinity. The lights are swinging over in this general direction now. You'll hear two explosions. There they are! That was the explosion overhead, not the guns themselves. I should think in a few minutes there may be a bit of shrapnel around here. Coming in – moving a little closer all the while. The plane is still very high. Earlier this evening we could hear occasional ... again those were explosions overhead. Earlier this evening we heard a number of bombs go sliding and slithering across to fall several blocks away. Just overhead now the burst of anti-aircraft fire. Still the near-by guns are not working. The searchlights now are feeling almost directly overhead. Now you'll hear two bursts a little nearer in a moment. There they are! That hard, stony sound.

October 1, 1940

Today, in one of the most famous streets in London, I saw soldiers at work clearing away the wreckage of nearly an entire block. The men were covered with white dust. Some of them wore goggles to protect their eyes. They thought, maybe, people were still buried in the basement. The sirens sounded, and still they tore at the beams and bricks covering the place where the basements used to be. They are still working tonight. I saw them after to-night's raid started. They paid no attention to the bursts of anti-aircraft fire overhead as they bent their backs and carried away basketfuls of mortar and brick. A few small steam-shovels would help them considerably in digging through those ruins. But all the modern instruments seem to be overhead. Down here on the ground people must work with their hands.

October 10, 1940

This is London, ten minutes before five in the morning. Tonight's raid has been widespread. London is again the main target. Bombs have been reported from more than fifty districts. Raiders have been over Wales in the west, the Midlands, Liverpool, the south-west, and north-east. So far as London is concerned, the outskirts appear to have suffered the heaviest pounding. The attack has decreased in intensity since the moon faded from the sky.

All the fires were quickly brought under control. That's a common phrase in the morning communiqués.[5] I've seen how it's done; spent a night with the London fire brigade. For three hours after the night attack got going, I shivered in a sandbag crow's-nest atop a tall building near the Thames. It was one of the many fire-observation posts. There was an old gun barrel mounted above a round table marked off like a compass. A stick of incendiaries[6] bounced off roof-tops about three miles away. The observer took a sight on a point where the first one fell, swung his gunsight along the line of bombs, and took another reading at the end of the line of fire. Then he picked up his telephone and shouted above the half gale that was blowing up there, 'Stick of incendiaries – between 190 and 220 – about three miles away.' Five minutes later a German bomber came boring down the river. We could see his exhaust trail like a pale ribbon stretched straight across the sky. Half a mile downstream there were two eruptions and then a third, close together. The first two looked as though some giant had thrown a huge basket of flaming golden oranges high in the air. The third was just a balloon of fire enclosed in black smoke above the house-tops. The observer didn't bother with his gun sight and indicator for that one. Just reached for his night glasses, took one quick look, picked up his telephone, and said, 'Two high explosives and one oil bomb,' and named the street where they had fallen.

---

[5] **communiqués:** official news messages
[6] **incendiaries:** fire bombs

There was a small fire going off to our left. Suddenly sparks showered up from it as though someone had punched the middle of a huge camp-fire with a tree trunk. Again the gun sight swung around, the bearing was read, and the report went down the telephone lines, 'There is something in high explosives on that fire at 59.'

There was peace and quiet inside for twenty minutes. Then a shower of incendiaries came down far in the distance. They didn't fall in a line. It looked like flashes from an electric train on a wet night, only the engineer was drunk and driving his train in circles through the streets. One sight at the middle of the flashes and our observer reported laconically,[7] 'Breadbasket at 90 – covers a couple of miles.' Half an hour later a string of fire bombs fell right beside the Thames. Their white glare was reflected in the black, lazy water near the banks and faded out in midstream where the moon cut a golden swathe broken only by the arches of famous bridges.

We could see little men shovelling those fire bombs into the river. One burned for a few minutes like a beacon right in the middle of a bridge. Finally those white flames all went out. No one bothers about the white light, it's only when it turns yellow that a real fire has started.

I must have seen well over a hundred fire bombs come down and only three small fires were started. The incendiaries aren't so bad if there is someone there to deal with them, but those oil bombs present more difficulties.

As I watched those white fires flame up and die down, watched the yellow blazes grow dull and disappear, I thought, what a puny effort is this to burn a great city. Finally, we went below to a big room under-ground. It was quiet. Women spoke softly into telephones. There was a big map of London on the wall. Little coloured pins were being moved from one point to another and every time a pin was moved it meant the

---

[7] **laconically:** with few words

fire pumps were on their way through the black streets of London to a fire.

We picked a fire from the map and drove to it. And the map was right. It was a small fire in a warehouse near the river. Not much of a fire; only ten pumps working on it, but still big enough to be seen from the air. The searchlights were bunched overhead and as we approached we could hear the drone of a German plane and see the burst of anti-aircraft fire directly overhead. Two pieces of shrapnel slapped down in the water and then everything was drowned in the hum of the pumps and the sound of hissing water. Those firemen in their oilskins and tin hats appeared oblivious[8] to everything but the fire. We went to another blaze – just a two-storey house down in the East End. An incendiary had gone through the roof and the place was being gutted. A woman stood on a corner, clutching a rather dirty pillow. A policeman was trying to comfort her. And a fireman said, 'You'd be surprised what strange things people pick up when they run out of a burning house.'

And back at headquarters I saw a man laboriously and carefully copying names in a big ledger – the list of firemen killed in action during the last month. There were about a hundred names.

I can now appreciate what lies behind those lines in the morning communiqués – all fires were quickly brought under control.

November 18, 1940
The other night – it might have been any wet night in mid-November – I heard a sound as I stood on a street corner. It was dark – time for the night raid to start. There was no traffic in the street. Big raindrops shattered themselves against the wooden paving blocks. The sound that I heard was caused by the raindrops, but they were not hitting the pavement. It was a crisp, bouncing sound. Some of you have heard that

---

[8] **oblivious:** unaware

sound as the rain drummed on a tent roof. Three people, old people they were, stood beside me in the rain and murk; they were on their way to the shelters. The bedding-rolls were hunched high on their shoulders, and the blankets and pillows were wrapped in oilcloth. As those three people squelched away in the darkness, looking like repugnant, hump-backed monsters, I couldn't help thinking after all they're rather lucky – there are hundreds of thousands who haven't even oilcloth to wrap their bedding-rolls.

Sounds, as well as words, get all twisted in wartime. Familiar harm-less sounds take on a sinister meaning. And, for me, the sound of rain-drops hitting windowpanes, tar roofs, or tents will always bring back those three misshapen people on a London street corner on a wet November night.

Activities

Close study (radio reportage: non-fiction recount text)

1 Murrow was famous for his sharp observation. Which details of things he has noticed bring these scenes to life?

2 Tiny sketches of people enliven the Blitz scenes. Make a list of these. Which do you find most memorable?

3 Where does he show his admiration for British people enduring the Blitz?

4 Murrow was necessarily discreet about horrors and deaths. Where does he hint at these?

5 He moves from general description to very close-up detail of a particular scene. What is so impressive about his final picture of people going to the shelters?

Language study

6 Comparisons are a key part of Murrow's descriptive power. Collect a variety of these from the passage. Which are most impressive?

7 Reread from 'I was up here earlier … ' to 'That hard, stony sound.' Why does Murrow use the present tense for verbs in this paragraph? Which of his senses is most used here? Pick out and comment on the comparisons. Why does he use short or broken sentences?

Writing

8 See page 128 for a question on this and the following passage.

Resources

Websites www.otr.com/murrow.html

Blitz Casualties

Frances Faviell from *A Chelsea Concerto* (1959)

In September, 1940, Frances Faviell was a VAD (Voluntary Aid Detachment) nurse working at a Chelsea hospital in London. Looking back on her Blitz experiences some eighteen years later, when the restraints of propaganda had been removed, she was frank about the horrors of the bombing and the grim tasks she had to perform.

The bomb and everyone's special bomb was still a subject of endless interest and possibilities – but they were coming so thick and fast that everyone had a better story than his neighbour. All over London people were full of stories of the Blitz, but life was going on as usual – in spite of it. September 14th was a date which few of the personnel at Post Don will forget. In a further day-light raid another shelter was hit – this time under a church. The Church of the Holy Redeemer is a massive building and I had been there several times to see the shelter in the crypt[1] because some of our refugees liked the idea of this shelter so much that they wanted to change to it. It was very close to Cheyne Hospital and when, at first, two of them did go there, I had gone to see that they were all right; but we persuaded them that it was too far and that their own was just as safe. It was a very popular shelter – perhaps because, like the refugees, others felt that nowhere would they be safer than under the protection of the Church – and at the time the bomb fell it was crowded.

The bomb was recorded by one of us telephonists in the Control Centre at 18.35. The message said that there was fire and casualties trapped in Holy Redeemer Church in Upper Cheyne Row. Requests followed in rapid succession for ambulances, blankets to cover the dead, fire services, and reports came in that there were many casualties.

---

[1] **crypt:** vault beneath a church

The bomb had struck the church at an angle through a window in a most extraordinary way and had penetrated the floor and burst among the shelterers, mostly women and small children. Here George Thorpe, whom we knew as 'Bert', lost his life with those women and children whom he had visited to reassure them – as he always did, although he was not the shelter warden. He knew that they were apt to become nervous and needed moral support in the heavy raids and he used to drop in there to boost up their courage and cheer them up. He had just despatched Jo Oakman on duty and gone there when the bomb fell. The bomb exploded right amongst the shelterers. A woman who was in the shelter told me about it when I visited her afterwards in St Luke's Hospital. She was badly injured and said that the scene resembled a massacre – in fact, she compared it to an engraving she had seen of the massacre of the women and children of Cawnpore in the Indian Mutiny,[2] with bodies, limbs, blood, and flesh mingled with little hats, coats, and shoes and all the small necessities which people took to the shelters with them. She said that people were literally blown to pieces and the mess was appalling. She herself was behind a pillar or buttress which protected her somewhat; and there was a pile of bodies between her and the explosion for it was still day-light – no one had gone to their bunks.

Jo and Len Lansdell were quickly at the scene, followed by all the ARP[3] Services. They could not get into the crypt at first because the body of a very heavy woman barred the only entrance. The explosion had set fire to the great heaps of coke stored there for heating the church and the smoke from it made it very difficult to see. Jo and Len Lansdell immediately set to work with stirrup pumps to try to extinguish it before the whole place became a crematorium. The body of Bert lay there face downwards. Jo, who had spoken to him only a few minutes before the

---

[2] **Indian Mutiny:** uprising against British rule in India, 1857–8. A British garrison of soldiers, women and children was slaughtered at Kanpur in 1857.

[3] **ARP:** air raid precautions

bomb fell, turned him over. She said afterwards that she wished so much that she hadn't, so that she could have remembered him as he had been when he had sent her on duty. His equipment, which was taken back to his post, was described to me as being bright red with blood – as was everything which had been in that crypt.

The work of the ARP Services that night was magnificent – by nine o'clock in the evening the casualties were all extricated and were laid in the grounds of the church with the Home Guard in charge …

▶ After a heavy raid with many casualties such as this one there was a task for which we were sometimes detailed from our FAP[4] and to which both our Commandants disliked having to send us. This was to help piece the bodies together in preparation for burial. The bodies – or rather the pieces – were in temporary mortuaries. It was a grim task and Betty Compton felt that we were too young and inexperienced for such a terrible undertaking – but someone had to do it and we were sent in pairs when it became absolutely necessary. Betty asked me if I would go as I had studied anatomy at the Slade. The first time I went my partner was a girl I did not know very well called Sheila. It *was* pretty grim, although it was all made as business-like and rapid as possible. We had somehow to form a body for burial so that the relatives (without seeing it) could imagine that their loved one was more or less intact for that purpose. But it was a very difficult task – there were so many pieces missing and, as one of the mortuary attendants said, 'Proper jig-saw puzzle, ain't it, Miss?' The stench was the worst thing about it – that, and having to realise that these frightful pieces of flesh had once been living, breathing people. We went out to smoke a cigarette when we simply could not go on – and some busybody saw Sheila smoking and reported her for smoking when in uniform and on duty. Betty Compton, who invariably supported her VADs, was most indignant about this, as indeed she was about us

---

[4] **FAP:** first aid post

having to perform such a task at all. I thought myself that butchers should have done it.

After the first violent revulsion I set my mind on it as a detached systematic task. It became a grim and ghastly satisfaction when a body was fairly constructed – but if one was too lavish in making one body almost whole then another one would have sad gaps. There were always odd members which did not seem to fit and there were too many legs. Unless we kept a very firm grip on ourselves nausea[5] was inevitable. The only way for me to stand it was to imagine that I was back in the anatomy class again – but there the legs and arms on which we studied muscles had been carefully preserved in spirit and were difficult to associate with the human body at all. I think that this task dispelled for me the idea that human life is valuable – it could be blown to pieces by blast – just as dust was blown by wind. The wardens had to gather up pieces after a bad raid – they had no choice – and someone had to assemble them into shrouds for Christian burial, but it seemed monstrous that these human beings had been reduced to this revolting indignity by other so-called Christians, and that we were doing the same in Germany and other countries. The feeling uppermost in my mind after every big raid was *anger*, anger at the lengths to which humans could go to inflict injury on one another. ◄

---

[5] ***nausea:*** sickness

Activities

Close study (memoir: non-fiction recount text)

1 Why was the Church shelter popular? How exactly did the bomb enter it and cause so much damage? What horrors did the rescuers find?

2 Piecing the bodies together was terrible work. Why was Frances Faviell chosen? How did she, and other people, try to make light of or endure the task?

3 What are the writer's final feelings about war in Christian Europe?

Language study

4 Reread from 'After a heavy raid ... ' (page 126) to the end. Which words and phrases convey the horror of sorting the body parts? Which express a grim light-heartedness?

Writing

5 (Extracts on pages 114–127) Write some entries of a civilian's diary of the Blitz in 1940.

6 (Extracts on pages 114–127) Compose an imaginative story about people involved in the bombing of the city. Use detail from the texts.

Reading

7 You might like to read the following eye-witness accounts of the bombing of London and other cities: *Blitz: The Civilian War: 1940–45* by Jane Waller and Michael Vaughan-Rees, *Waiting for the All Clear* by Ben Wicks.

Resources

Website www.museum.London.org.uk

Christmas Patrol

William Woodruff from *Vessel of Sadness* (1969)

*Born in Lancashire, William Woodruff (b.1916) left school at fourteen.
As he struggled to find work in London during the Great Depression of
the 1930s, he maintained a passion for self-education, which eventually
won him a place at Oxford University. From 1940–46 he served with the
British Army, surviving war's 'total madness' in fierce campaigns in Italy
and France. After the war he resumed his academic career, holding
professorships in economics at universities in the USA and Australia.*

*Vessel of Sadness (1969), from which the extract is taken, was
described by the writer J.B. Priestley as 'a remarkable book indeed, bringing us close to the huge face of war'. Woodruff aims to show 'the gut-
twisting fear of soldiers in battle'. He bases his story-like chapters on the
bloody Allied Italian campaign of 1943–5. Italy was Nazi Germany's
ally in the Second World War. US and British forces landed in southern
Italy in September, 1943, and advanced north. Even though Italy changed
sides and deposed its dictator, Mussolini, the German army held on,
blocking the Allied advance at Monte Cassino, where a fortified hill-top
monastery dominated the only road through the mountains. To bypass
this and so reach Rome, the Allies landed further north at Anzio in
January, 1944. A break-out was blocked by the Germans and heavy
fighting in the marshes near Anzio made a battlefield like those of the
First World War: 75,000 Allied troops were killed or wounded. These
Italian scenes provide the battlescapes of Woodruff's book. He presents
episodes from this 'insufferable event' with 'desolating realism'.*

*Woodruff shows the horror of the Cassino fighting by describing an
obscure incident, the meeting of two army patrols well away from the
main fighting. We share the thoughts of the men (known only by number
or rank) following Woodruff's intention 'to tell of war through the frag-
mented impressions in the minds of men'.*

★

A candle flickered in the corner of a stable on an Italian hillside; casting its moving shadows against the wall and among the darkened rafters. The cattle stalls were empty. A group of British soldiers were sitting on a pile of straw playing cards. Cigarette smoke rose above them. Someone was playing carols on a mouth organ. Outside was a snow-covered world and a starlit night. Great pointed icicles hung from the barn roof ready to fall into the yard below with the crash of glass. Except for a stray shell exploding in the distance all was quiet. Soldiers kept watch. Above them was the Abbey of Monte Cassino, the oldest monastery in Christendom. It was Christmas Eve, 1943.

A sergeant entered the stable and talked with a corporal lying on a straw-filled manger. The corporal muttered, rolled out of the manger, swore, and went into the adjoining room. The carol playing ceased, the laughter stopped.

'The patrol's on,' he said matter-of-factly. 'I'll need two of you.'

'Hasn't Sarge heard it's bloody Christmas Eve?'

'The war hasn't. The war's greedy.'

A bunch of matchsticks protruded from the top of the corporal's clenched fist.

'Shortest two goes.'

'Depart 2200 hours, check and briefing at 2100 hours. Nothing new about it: out by way of the bridge, along the river, up the creek, through the wood, around the bottom of 'Polski's hill', up and over Hangman's Hill, across the open ground to 'Lofty's farm' (they say the wolves took Lofty's body out and messed it about), then across the open ground to the woods, praying nobody's watching, then into cover, across the road at 'burnt-out corner' and home again. Just about the time that we go out,' he added, tucking his stocking cap into the back of his tunic, 'the Yanks will attack Hill 730. I'm not going to dispute my share of 730. It's a graveyard up there.'

'Rome by Christmas!' murmured the man shuffling the cards. 'The General must have been mad. It isn't reasonable to have so many mountains! I wonder if the travel posters are still on the wall outside Charing Cross station. "Come to Sunny Italy!" '

The corporal wriggled down into the straw again and continued to stare into the rafters. He didn't care about the war any more. He had almost reached the desperate stage when he wouldn't care about surviving. He had fought his way across North Africa. Then he had fought his way up here from Salerno. Through orange and lemon groves, through great stands of evergreens, sombre pines and great oaks. Then into the craggy mountains, through defile after defile; sometimes with the help of a mule; sometimes along mountain tracks where a mule couldn't go and the soldiers were the beasts of burden. Always onward it seemed, through fog and rain with little to eat and that stone cold. He'd been in the fight for the bridge at Scafati, where Richard had copped it. That's when something inside him had broken. A crowd of them had then crossed to the coast and struggled across the blue shoulder of Vesuvius.[1] From an observatory tower on the western slope of the mountain they had rested with their backs against chestnut saplings and had looked upon the immensity of sky and sea and mountain, disbelievingly.

There had been no rest when they got into Naples; they had rushed after Jerry to the Volturno. In pouring rain they had struggled to cross the river at Capua only to be driven back. The Yanks got across higher up. After that it was one hill after another – through little white-washed villages clinging to the mountainside like swallows' nests – until they'd reached the banks of the Garigliano. Outside one little place with a saint's name, they'd been met by a little group of black-dressed women, their hands pressed together in prayer, who had beseeched them to go away, that their village might be spared. It hadn't been spared. It was a

[1] **Vesuvius:** a volcano near Naples

queer little place; nailed at a drunken angle to the side of a ravine. It did what they had expected it to do. When Jerry put a barrage of heavy mortars down on its head the village gave up the ghost and slid into the ravine, children, grandmothers and all. They had cast the little bunches of mountain flowers which the women had given them after the train of ruin down the mountainside, sadly.

The laughter broke out again next door. The man with the mouth organ was having difficulty with 'Good King Wenceslas'. Somebody kicked on the door and bawled out 'Christmas Eve booze is up'. There was a scramble for mess tins, weapons and helmets.

A platoon sergeant carrying a sub-machine gun ran down the steps of a deep underground shelter in the vicinity of Monte Cassino. He drew back a heavy curtain concealing the entrance to a crowded, smoke-filled, ill-lit dugout.

'Achtung![2] Tonight's patrol will consist of the following ... ' He read nine names.

'Jawohl!'[3]

Some of the acknowledgements could hardly be heard.

In less than two minutes he had dropped the curtain back into position and was out in the snow-covered street. For a moment he looked up at the Abbey and the star-filled sky. He sniffed the cold air and listened. Somewhere in the vicinity of[4] a bombed church he heard the singing of 'Stille Nacht'.[5]

---

[2] **Achtung:** Attention! (German)
[3] **Jawohl:** yes (German)
[4] **in the vicinity of:** near to
[5] **'Stille Nacht':** 'Silent Night' (German)

'Here, mate, watch the wire. "Peace on earth" is the password, and for Christ's sake come back quietly. Good luck, chum.'

A British sentry standing by a snow-covered stone wall watched the patrol as it crossed the field and was swallowed up into the night. The sentry stamped his feet. Somebody said this was the worst Italian winter in living memory.

Nine men moved on in the darkness, silently, isolated, a little ship in a hostile sea. They passed through a gate thrown back across a dirt road, filed past a row of flattened mud huts which led to abandoned vegetable allotments. They then reached an open meadow. The first nervousness was passing. The hard tightness in the chest had eased off and the trickle of sweat down the spine had ceased. With luck, it would be no worse than the loss of another night's sleep.

The path dipped down towards the river. Normally there was a good deal of loose gravel here which made an awful noise under heavy boots – even when you wore socks over them to muffle the noise. Now the blanket of snow quietened the earth. The only sound was the crunch of snow as the men followed each other down the slight incline towards the water. It was quite dark and slightly warmer. The patrol shifted course to the right when the first clump of willows came into sight. Something squawked at the side of the water. There was a plop as an animal left the ice and entered the river.

The corporal had covered this ground a dozen times in the past two months. Usually he had followed the platoon sergeant, but tonight he was out on his own, in front. With the river on his left he felt happier about his bearings. One day from a forward post he had watched a heron standing in the shallows about here. Not long ago, curlews and peewits had risen from this meadow when a shell exploded. Two days ago, he had studied the bank of the river for hours through his glasses without seeing a bird of any kind.

The corporal slowed down until he was sure that all his men were with him. Without speaking he made off upstream. The others followed. Over on the right in the direction of Hill 730, a considerable battle was developing. The hills were silhouetted against the sky as the light cast by the shell explosions blinked on and off. A red flare rose and fell, giving the hillside a fiery glow. A great chandelier of light fell into the battle area turning night into day. The blinding light was reflected from the dark clouds above the mountains. That nasty woodpecker noise coming from the mountainside was German heavy machine guns. Quite deadly; one peck and men went down like lumps of wood, arms and legs sticking out in all directions. It made you afraid of all machines. The light machine gun that No. 8 carried, at the end of the section, was a peashooter compared to the 'heavy'.

There was a slight movement ahead and the corporal tensed himself and peered into the darkness. Something scurried across the snow. The patrol continued.

At the opening of a creek running inland across the meadow into the foothills the nine men halted to re-arrange their loads. For a few minutes they crouched on their haunches and listened. Except for the fighting on Hill 730 and some sporadic[6] shelling across the river there was no noise. The men spoke in the slightest whisper, faces close together. They took a short swig from the corporal's flask as a small plane hovered above their heads. Who knew, the plane might go slamming into the hillside. Anything, as long as it didn't drop a flare followed by a canister of bombs.

No. 2 didn't care whether the plane was friend or foe.

His face and hands were getting numb with cold. He cursed the snow, he cursed the war and he cursed the winter, especially this winter filled with rain and cold and mud and snow and death. Monte Camino had been his first real taste of fighting mud, rain and Germans. For ten

---

[6] **sporadic:** occasional

days on the slopes of Camino, he and his comrades had fought all three, and had been defeated by all three. Exhausted to the point of weeping they'd been dragged out of the line and plopped down in a wet meadow within sound of the guns. They'd been ordered to rest. Monte Camino was still there when they went back into action. It still blocked their path. It had rained so heavily that the General had called the next offensive 'Operation Raincoat'. The rain wasn't deceived, nor the mud, nor the Germans. His mob had almost perished on a hilltop called La Bandita. They'd fought all day to see whose hill it was. Then torrential rains had washed out the battle. He had spent the night standing huddled against another fellow in a hollow tree. The rains had stopped the next morning but by then they were like drowned rats and it was all they could do to bring in the wounded and bury the dead. It was from there, in November, that they got their first real look at Monastery Hill. They had been looking at it and fighting for it ever since. Monte Cassino was a door sealing the entrance to the Liri Valley, the Alban hills and the approaches to Rome. The Germans intended to keep it shut.

The patrol turned up the creek into the hills. Several more low-flying planes flew over in the direction of Hill 730. Explosions followed as the planes dropped anti-personnel bombs. In the dark it was like trucks tipping out loads of heavy stones. By the time the anti-aircraft guns had got into action the sound of the light planes had almost died away.

At the end of the section, No. 8 was dragging one of the legs of the machine-gun tripod through the snow, causing a snake-like furrow to follow him in the dark. No. 8 was listening to the explosions in the distance. He kept well up against No. 7. Where he could, he stepped into No. 7's footprints in the snow. It was easier that way. He watched the bowed head in front of him. He wondered what was going on in No. 7's head. But what did it matter what was going on in other people's heads? He followed his instincts. They'd got themselves into this pickle by people thinking too much. People who just sat and thought and thought, were like birds who sat and preened and preened, and who never used their feathers, or laid an egg. No. 8's ambition was to keep a full belly, stay safe, get home and at all costs avoid the thinkers. What price thinking when it landed you on a perishing hillside, on a Christmas Eve, far from home with the fear of death inside you?

For some time now the patrol had trudged along – nine men lost in their own little world. They had followed the creek until it ran into the wood. They had avoided the intersections and had crossed the lanes among the trees quickly. From the edge of the wood they had climbed 'Polski's hill'. For a week or two this hill had been inhabited by an unhinged Polish soldier who, from a lair, rained death on anybody who passed by. Polski had foxed both sides. He should not have been there, and the clown did not distinguish between friend or foe. In time, he had run out of ammunition and had marched back to his battalion across a minefield in the pitch dark singing his head off. The Poles had packed him off somewhere without a scratch on him. 'Doing a Polski' was a phrase already being used by the soldiers for anybody who managed to avoid the reaper by acting daft.

After 'Polski's hill' they climbed up Hangman's Hill. The going was tougher up the hillside and they halted now and again to get their breath. It was when they got up there that the snowstorm began. It began slowly. No more than the odd flake striking the eye. Later, a cascade of starshells falling upon Monte Cassino revealed the Abbey silhouetted against a snow-filled sky.

No. 7 was oblivious to the snowstorm. His mind was fixed on a pathetic little airmail letter in his pocket. It was from his wife telling him she had been unfaithful and was about to bear a child. It had been snowing gently when he'd got the letter earlier in the day. He'd stood in the farmyard with the other fellows around the post corporal laughing and joking as they'd got their letters. When he had read the first few lines he had found it difficult to understand what his wife was trying to say, and he had started at the beginning again. Slowly the truth had borne in upon him. There was to be a child, of his wife, her first child, but not of him.

For a little while he'd leant against the barn wall holding the letter before him, reading it, rereading it. The snowflakes had thawed on the notepaper causing the ink to run. But the ink had run in parts of the letter where the snow had never fallen. They were his wife's tears. Later he had thought he was going to go mad if he didn't tell somebody what had happened, so he had told his mate. His mate had looked at him for a long time queerly and then he said, 'Look Bernie, your missus isn't the only one in England with a bun in the oven.'

It was 3 am on Christmas Day. There was still heavy fighting on Hill 730. A blizzard was blowing. It had snowed heavily since midnight. The snow now came in great blinding gusts. The patrol had halted close to 'Lofty's farm'. They were huddled together in the lee of a wall. The corporal was peering in the direction of the farm, brushing the snow out of his eyes. He was worried. Should he get into 'Lofty's farm' and stay there until darkness returned again? Or should he dig in here against the wall? Or should he make a run home on a compass bearing? All they had to do was to keep their backs to the din coming from Hill 730 and follow their noses. They would be sure to strike the river. He knew how to cut corners in this country. The more the corporal thought, the more confident he became that he could get his team home even allowing for the blizzard and the depth of the snow. Battalion knew of his predicament and would help him with radio. Only trouble with the emergency system was that Jerry knew all about it, too. Jerry sometimes tagged on and came home with you, knocking you off just when you'd got cocky and careless and were about to duck through your own wire. It was dangerous. But then sitting out here was dangerous too. And it was Christmas Day.

There was more quiet talking among the group sheltering in the lee of the wall. Suddenly the corporal got up from where he was crouched.

'All right,' he said quietly, 'let's go home then. We'll have to bunch up and we'll have to move.'

There was a last little drop of rum in his flask. He drank it. Then he left the protection of the wall and the others filed after him. The snow-filled wind now broke over the patrol like a giant wave. It hurled itself upon them, driving a great white spray through their open legs as they marched. It tugged at their clothing, buffeted them, raced and swirled around them like a spinning top, blinding them.

▶ The German saw the British corporal first. He fired, taking off the top of the corporal's head. Two seconds later both leaders were lying in the snow dying. Terror seized both sides: there were shots, shouts. Six or seven bodies fell almost at once. A few Germans ploughed their way back to the shelter of the wood and four of the British scrambled through the snow towards the wall they had just left, the fear of death upon them. The snow soon lay trampled and bloodstained. Deep foot-prints radiated across the hillside. Patches of snow were already dyed deep red. A trail of blood ran to the edge of the wood. One man almost gained the shelter of the trees only to topple over into the deep snow. He raised himself up and then fell back again, as if the effort was not worthwhile.

Somewhere in the wood a wounded man was calling, a howling wind drowning his cries. A single shot rang through the hills across the snow. Abandoned equipment lay everywhere. The snow continued to fall in great puffs. The branches of the evergreens sank closer to the earth.

The dawn of Christmas Day, 1943. The blizzard had passed. The rising sun caused the cedars to cast their long shadows before them. On Hangman's Hill a rabbit was scratching at the deep snow trying to reach the soil below. A glistening white blanket covered the earth. Only the red holly berries stood in contrast to the whiteness of the snow. From the wood the calls of a wounded man were heard, weakly and infrequently. In the Christian world they were celebrating the birth of Christ. On the skyline, in the candle-lit, refugee-crowded chapel of the Monastery of Monte Cassino, an old priest wearing his vestments[7] ascended the altar, arms outstretched, to say the first Christ mass. ◄

---

[7] **vestments:** religious robes

Activities

Close study (semi-fiction: narrative text)

1 What are the corporal's memories of war in Italy? Which incident was the most tragic?

2 Why is the second section, about the German patrol, ironic?

3 Outline the thoughts of the corporal, No. 2, No. 8 and No. 7 as they move forward on patrol.

4 The climax of the episode (pages 138–139) is the shock of the contact between patrols. What exactly happens? Who survives?

5 There are many references to the Biblical Christmas nativity story. Find some of these. How does Woodruff contrast what happens in the story with Christmas and the Christian beliefs suggested in its background? (Note: The monastery was destroyed by bombing in January, 1944.)

Language study

6 The impressive climax to the story is full of bold contrasts. Find ten words or phrases related to violence, and ten related to beauty and peace.

7 Where and how are sounds used to enrich the fine visual description? Why are the following words and phrases impressive?
  • 'the fear of death upon them'
  • 'the red holly berries stood in contrast to the whiteness of the snow'
  • 'weakly and infrequently'
  • 'refugee-crowded'
  • 'arms outstretched'.

Writing

8 Tell the story through the eyes of one of the other men on the patrol, or one of the Germans.

9 The First World War was remarkable for its Christmas truces of 1914 and 1915 when both sides stopped fighting on the Western Front. Read this letter by a Scottish officer, Sir Edward Hulse (1890–1915). He describes the truce in Flanders.

> ... at 10 am I was surprised to hear a hell of a din going on, and not a single man left in my trenches; they were completely denuded (against my orders), and nothing lived! I heard strains of 'Tipperary' floating down the breeze, swiftly followed by a tremendous burst of 'Deutschland über Alles', and as I got to my own Coy. H.-qrs. dug-out, I saw, to my amazement, not only a crowd of about 150 British and Germans at the half-way house which I had appointed opposite my lines, but six or seven such crowds, all the way down our lines.

Scots and Huns were fraternising in the most genuine possible manner. Every sort of souvenir was exchanged, addresses given and received, photos of families shown, etc.

A German NCO with the Iron Cross – gained, he told me, for conspicuous skill in sniping – started his fellows off on some marching tune. When they had done I set the note for 'The Boys of Bonnie Scotland, where the heather and the bluebells grow,' and so we went on, singing everything from 'Good King Wenceslaus' down to the ordinary Tommies' song, and ended up with 'Auld Lang Syne', which we all, English, Scots, Irish, Prussian, Wurtembergers, etc., joined in. It was absolutely astounding, and if I had seen it on a cinematograph film I should have sworn that it was faked! ...

From foul rain and wet, the weather had cleared up the night before to a sharp frost, and it was a perfect day, everything white, and the silence seemed extraordinary, after the usual din. From all sides birds seemed to arrive, and we hardly ever see a bird generally. Later in the day I fed about 50 sparrows outside my dug-out, which shows how complete the silence and quiet was.

Contrast *Christmas Patrol* with this Christmas truce letter. What happens in each? Discuss:
• the attitude of soldiers to each other
• the concept of Christmas
• the use of nature as a contrast to war.

Reading
10 Other fine prose books on the Second World War, written by soldiers, that you might like to read include *Fleshwounds* by David Holbrook (D-Day) and *Alamein to Zem-Zem* by Keith Douglas (war in the Libyan desert).

Nuclear Attack

The principles of an atomic bomb were worked out by the 1930s. In the USA, Albert Einstein, a German Jewish scientist driven into exile by the Nazis, wrote to President Roosevelt in 1939, urging him to develop the weapon before the Germans did. American and British scientific teams worked on the secret 'Manhattan Project' at Los Alamos in New Mexico. At a cost of 500 million dollars, an atomic bomb was detonated in the nearby desert on 17 July, 1945. The military rushed the weapon into action in the war against the Japanese.

Harry Truman, the new President, feared the human cost of an invasion of Japan and wished to end the war swiftly. On 6 August, 1945, the 'Enola Gay', a B29 bomber, with two escorts, flew to Japan from the Marianas islands, an American Pacific base. The 'Enola Gay' carried an atomic bomb, 'Little Boy'. Its target was Hiroshima, a city previously untouched by American air raids.

At 8.15 am the bomb was dropped, floating down by parachute until it exploded 2000 feet above the city centre. The aircraft commander saw a 'bright light', then a 'rolling and boiling cloud' with 'a fiery red core.

In the city, survivors remembered 'blinding, intense light'. At the epicentre of the explosion, heat incinerated people so completely that only their shadows remained, burned into pavements or walls. Blast reduced everything to rubble. Fire destroyed what remained. It is thought that 200,000 people died as a result of the bombing.

Resources for pages 142–150

Books *Hiroshima* by John Hersey (stories of several survivors)
Hiroshima edited by Adrian Weekes (background and eye-witness material)
Website www.csi.ad.jp/ABOMB/ (gives information on both 1945 attacks and invites peace messages which are floated down the Hiroshima rivers on 6 August)

Hiroshima After the Bomb

Marcel Junod from *Warrior Without Weapons* (1951)

Marcel Junod, a French doctor working for the International Red Cross, was sent into Hiroshima a month after the bomb fell. From the aircraft he saw the city as 'a huge white patch ... This chalk desert, looking almost like ivory in the sun, surrounded by a crumble of twisted ironwork and ash heaps, was all that remained of Hiroshima'.

Early on September 9th the investigation commission left the island of Miyajima. From our hotel we walked along the shore to the little harbour. In the soft and diffused light of the early morning, the gilded pediments[1] of the temple gate were lapped by the incoming tide. We boarded the boat which was to take us over the arm of sea which separated us from the main island.

A car was waiting for us there and I sat between two Japanese interpreters, a Miss Ito, who had been born in Canada, and a Japanese journalist who had spent twenty years in the United States. They both gave me a great deal of information about what Hiroshima had once been: its main activities and its geographical situation. I needed their accounts to compare the reality of yesterday, a busy prosperous town, with the reality of today: the desolating spectacle after its utter destruction by one flash of blinding searing[2] light.

'Hiroshima,' explained the fragile Miss Ito in her blue kimono,[3] 'means "the broad island"'. It was built on the delta of the river Ota which flows down from Mount Kamuri, and it was the seventh town in point of size in Japan. The seven arms of the Oto – seven rivers which pour their waters into the inland sea – enclose in an almost perfect triangle the harbour of

---

[1] **pediments:** triangular upper parts
[2] **searing:** scorching
[3] **kimono:** Japanese robe

the town, the factories, an arsenal, oil refineries and warehouses. Hiroshima had a population of 250,000 people and, in addition, there was a garrison of about 150,000 soldiers.

The journalist described the main official buildings of the town, which were built with reinforced concrete and dominated a sea of low-roofed Japanese houses extending over six miles to the wooded hill I could see in the distance.

'The town was not much damaged,' he explained. 'It had suffered very little from bombing. There were only two minor raids, one on March 19th last by a squadron of American naval planes, and one on April 30th by a Flying Fortress.

'On August 6th there wasn't a cloud in the sky above Hiroshima, and a mild, hardly perceptible wind blew from the south. Visibility was almost perfect for ten or twelve miles.

'At nine minutes past seven in the morning an air-raid warning sounded and four[4] American B29 planes appeared. To the north of the town two of them turned and made off to the south and disappeared in the direction of the Shoho Sea. The other two, after having circled the neighbourhood of Shukai, flew off at high speed southwards in the direction of the Bingo Sea.

'At 7.31 the all-clear was given. Feeling themselves in safety people came out of their shelters and went about their affairs and the work of the day began.

'Suddenly a glaring whitish pinkish light appeared in the sky accompanied by an unnatural tremor which was followed almost immediately by a wave of suffocating heat and a wind which swept away everything in its path.

'Within a few seconds the thousands of people in the streets and the gardens in the centre of the town were scorched by a wave of searing

---

[4] **four:** there were actually three

heat. Many were killed instantly, others lay writhing[5] on the ground screaming in agony from the intolerable pain of their burns. Everything standing upright in the way of the blast, walls, houses, factories and other buildings, was annihilated and the debris spun round in a whirl-wind and was carried up into the air. Trams were picked up and tossed aside as though they had neither weight nor solidity. Trains were flung off the rails as though they were toys. Horses, dogs and cattle suffered the same fate as human beings. Every living thing was petrified[6] in an attitude of indescribable suffering. Even the vegetation did not escape. Trees went up in flames, the rice plants lost their greenness, the grass burned on the ground like dry straw.

'Beyond the zone of utter death in which nothing remained alive houses collapsed in a whirl of beams, bricks and girders. Up to about three miles from the centre of the explosion lightly built houses were flattened as though they had been built of cardboard. Those who were inside were either killed or wounded. Those who managed to extricate themselves[7] by some miracle found themselves surrounded by a ring of fire. And the few who succeeded in making their way to safety generally died twenty or thirty days later from the delayed effects of the deadly gamma rays. Some of the reinforced concrete or stone buildings remained standing but their interiors were completely gutted by the blast.

'About half an hour after the explosion whilst the sky all around Hiroshima was still cloudless a fine rain began to fall on the town and went on for about five minutes. It was caused by the sudden rise of over-heated air to a great height, where it condensed and fell back as rain. Then a violent wind rose and the fires extended with terrible rapidity, because most Japanese houses are built only of timber and straw.

---

[5] **writhing:** twisting about

[6] **petrified:** turned to stone

[7] **extricate themselves:** get out

'By the evening the fire began to die down and then it went out. There was nothing left to burn. Hiroshima had ceased to exist.'

The Japanese broke off and then pronounced one word with indescribable but restrained emotion:

'Look.'

We were then rather less than four miles away from the Aioi Bridge, which was immediately beneath the explosion, but already the roofs of the houses around us had lost their tiles and the grass was yellow along the roadside. At three miles from the centre of the devastation the houses were already destroyed, their roofs had fallen in and the beams jutted out from the wreckage of their walls. But so far it was only the usual spectacle presented by towns damaged by ordinary high explosives.

About two and a half miles from the centre of the town all the buildings had been burnt out and destroyed. Only traces of the foundations and piles of debris and rusty charred ironwork were left. This zone was like the devastated areas of Tokio, Osaka and Kobé after the mass fall of incendiaries.[8]

At three-quarters of a mile from the centre of the explosion nothing at all was left. Everything had disappeared. It was a stony waste littered with debris and twisted girders. The incandescent breath of the fire had swept away every obstacle and all that remained upright were one or two fragments of stone walls and a few stoves which had remained incongruously on their base.

We got out of the car and made our way slowly through the ruins into the centre of the dead city. Absolute silence reigned in the whole necropolis.[9] There was not even a survivor searching in the ruins, though some distance away a group of soldiers were clearing a passage through the debris. Here and there a little grass was beginning to

---

[8] *incendiaries:* fire bombs

[9] *necropolis:* cemetery

sprout amidst the ruins, but there was not a bird or an animal to be seen anywhere.

Professor Tsusuki led the way and spoke in a loud voice so that we could all hear what he said. His sentences came to us disjointed as though by deep excitement and emotion.

'We must open our minds ... We must try to understand everything.'

He pointed to the remnants of wall, the base of which ran for perhaps six or seven yards.

'There was a hospital here, gentlemen. Two hundred beds, eight doctors, twenty nurses. Every single one and all the patients were killed. Never mind. What does it matter. That's what an atomic bomb does.'

Sometimes I could catch only the last words of a sentence:

' ... open our minds ... so much to say. Let's go on to other things.

'Here's a half-destroyed bank. Employees from another town came here two days after the explosion. They spent the night in a room which had a metal curtain rail and silk curtains. They are both down with pernicious anaemia[10] ... '.

Whilst the American physicists took more notes and used their detecting instruments to make quite certain that all radiation had ceased Dr Tsusuki led his fellow doctors to the hospitals. It was there that the most terrible sights of all awaited us.

These 'hospitals' had been set up on the outskirts of the town in the rare buildings which had escaped complete destruction and were regarded as 'less damaged'. Even if there was no roof and only the walls standing, scores and sometimes even hundreds of wounded had been carried there. There were no beds, no water, no medical supplies and no proper medical attention.

The first of these places visited was installed in a former school which had been only partly demolished. Eighty patients were stretched out on

---

[10] ***pernicious anaemia:*** sickness of blood

the bare floor and there was nothing to protect them from the rain or the chill air of the nights. In many cases their wounds were still unbound and clouds of flies had settled on them. A few pots of ointment were ranged on a shelf. Substitute bandages had been made out of some coarse material. That was all the medical attention half a dozen nurses assisted by perhaps a dozen or so girls whose ages ranged from twelve to fifteen, could give their patients.

Professor Tsusuki was now talking of the patients as he had previously talked of the ruins. He pointed to one woman, who was only semi-conscious. The flames had disfigured her face.

'Infection of the blood,' he observed dryly. 'White corpuscles almost entirely destroyed. Gamma rays. Nothing to be done about it. She'll be dead this evening or tomorrow. That's what an atomic bomb does.'

We visited dozens of such improvised hospitals as well as the hospital of the Japanese Red Cross Society, which was ultra-modern. It had no glass in any of its windows now and all its laboratory apparatus had been put out of commission. Six hundred out of a thousand patients had died in the first few days and been buried somehow in the neighbourhood of the hospital.

One could go on indefinitely describing the horror of it all; the thousands of helpless, suffering bodies stretched out on the ground; the thousands of swollen charred faces; the ulcerated backs; the suppurating[11] arms raised up in order to avoid contact with any covering.

And each one of those human beings represented an infinity of suffering. Those disfigured masks would always retain the horror of what they had witnessed. What must they have been thinking when they saw the neat American uniforms passing through their ranks?

A young Japanese doctor accompanied me to the train when I left to return to Tokio.

---

[11] **suppurating:** festering

On what remained of the station façade[12] the hands of the clock had been stopped by the fire at 8.15.

It was perhaps the first time in the history of humanity that the birth of a new era was recorded on the face of a clock.

---

[12] ***façade:*** frontage

Activities

Close study (memoir: non-fiction recount text)

1 How does the opening paragraph contrast with what follows?
2 What is the point of Miss Ito's introduction to the city?
3 What are the most dramatic and horrible parts of the journalist's story of the bombing?
4 Why is the single word 'Look' so effective?
5 How does the damage get worse as you approach the city centre?
6 What is the sinister long-term effect of the bomb on its victims?
7 Why is the clock time so dramatic at the end?

Language study

8 Junod writes cleverly of the increasing devastation as the visitors draw near the centre of the city. Trace the phrases that indicate the different stages of this exploration. Which sentences show the climax of this journey?
9 How does Junod use times and distances to define the drama of Hiroshima? How does he use contrast, especially of the living and the dead, to show his horror at the bombing?

The Nagasaki Atom Bomb

After Hiroshima, despite massive propaganda by the Allies, the Japanese High Command stubbornly refused to give in. The entry of the Soviet Union into the war against Japan forced the Americans to carry out another nuclear mission. On 8 August, another B29, named 'Bock's Car', set off, carrying a second, larger atomic bomb, 'Fat Man'. Bad weather allowed the primary target, Kokura, to escape. Cloud broke to give a clear view of Nagasaki, the secondary target.

The bomb exploded at 11.02 am. Astonished aircrew saw 'a giant pillar of purple fire ... shooting skywards', and then turning into a huge mushroom-shaped cloud 'seething and boiling in a white fury of creamy foam'.

Although the second bomb was more powerful than 'Little Boy', the hills around Nagasaki seemed to restrict casualties to some 70,000. Tatsuichiro Akizuki, a Japanese doctor, worked at a tuberculosis hospital about a mile from the epicentre of the explosion. He lived to write a striking description of the attack.

Tatsuichiro Akizuki from *Nagasaki 1945* (1981)

On Thursday, 9 August, the boundless blue sky, the loud shrilling of cicadas,[1] promised another day as hot and as sultry as the day before.

At 8.30 I began the medical examination and treatment of out-patients. Nearly thirty had turned up by ten o'clock. Some were patients requiring artificial pneumo-thorax (the temporary collapsing of a lung); they had been entrusted to us by Takahara Hospital, 5000 metres away. Miss Yoshioka, a woman doctor in her mid-thirties who came from there, arrived to assist me with the operations, as well as two nurses also belonging to Takahara Hospital. Our hospital was in something of a turmoil.

---

[1] *cicadas:* crickets

During the morning Mr Yokota turned up to see his daughter, who was one of our in-patients. He lived at the foot of Motohara Hill, and was an engineer in the research department of the Mitsubishi Ordnance Factory, then one of the centres of armament manufacture in Japan. The torpedoes used in the attack on Pearl Harbor[2] had been made there. Mr Yokota always had something interesting to say. He used to visit me now and again, often passing on some new piece of scientific information.

He said: 'I hear Hiroshima was very badly damaged on the sixth.'

Together we despaired over the destiny of Japan, he as an engineer, I as a doctor.

Then he said gloomily: 'I don't think the explosion was caused by any form of chemical energy.'

'What then?' I inquired, eager to know about the cause of the explosion, even though my patients were waiting for me.

He said: 'The power of the bomb dropped on Hiroshima is far stronger than any accumulation of chemical energy produced by the dissolution of a nitrogen compound, such as nitro-glycerine. It was an *atomic* bomb, produced by atomic fission.'[3]

'Good heavens! At last we have atomic fission!' I said, though somewhat doubtfully.

Just then the long continuous wail of a siren arose.

'Listen ... Here comes the regular air-raid.'

'The first warning ... The enemy is on their way.'

Mr Yokota hurried back down the hill to his factory and all at once I began to feel nervous. It was now about 10.30. When such a warning sounded we were supposed to make sure our patients took refuge in our basement air-raid shelter. We were meant to do likewise. But recently I had become so accustomed to air-raids that, even though it was somewhat foolhardy, I no longer bothered with every precaution. In any case,

---

[2] **Pearl Harbor:** American naval base (attacked by the Japanese in December 1941)

[3] **atomic fission:** splitting of the atom

breakfast was about to begin. At the time our diet at the hospital consisted of two meals a day of unpolished rice. The patients were waiting for their breakfast to be served, and so remained on the second and third floors.

I went out of the building. It was very hot. The sky had clouded over a little but the familiar formation of B29 bombers was neither to be seen nor heard. I asked myself: 'What route will our dear enemies choose to take today?'

I went in again to warn my patients to stay away from the windows – they could be swept by machine-gun fire. Recently we had been shot up once or twice by fighter-planes from American aircraft carriers in neighbouring waters.

About thirty minutes later the all-clear sounded. I said to myself: In Nagasaki everything is still all right. *Im Westen Nichts Neues* – All quiet on the Western Front.

I went down to the consulting room, humming cheerfully. Now that the all-clear had been given I felt free from danger. I entered the room and found Dr Yoshioka about to carry out an artificial pneumo-thorax operation on one of the male out-patients. 'You ought to stop working when the air-raid warning goes, at least for a little while,' I told her.

'Thank you,' she replied. 'But there were so many patients waiting.'

She looked tired. She had come to the hospital that morning on foot, walking 5000 metres across Nagasaki, and since then she had been very busy treating the patients who needed attention.

'Please have a rest,' I said. 'I'll carry on in your place.'

'Well ... Thank you for your kindness,' she said, and went upstairs to her room to rest. I began the pneumo-thorax. Miss Sugako Murai, one of our few trained nurses, was there by my side to help me. She was two years younger than me and came from Koshima in Nagasaki; she had been at Urakami Hospital for about four months, since April.

It was eleven o'clock. The hospital was a hive of activity after the all-clear.

'Well, we'll soon be getting our breakfast,' I said to Miss Murai. 'The patients must be hungry.'

So was I, but before we had our breakfast we would have to finish treating all the out-patients.

I stuck the pneumo-thorax needle into the side of the chest of the patient lying on the bed. It was just after 11 am.

I heard a low droning sound, like that of distant aeroplane engines.

'What's that?' I said. 'The all-clear has gone, hasn't it?'

At the same time the sound of the plane's engines, growing louder and louder, seemed to swoop down over the hospital.

I shouted: 'It's an enemy plane! Look out – take cover!'

As I said so, I pulled the needle out of the patient and threw myself beside the bed.

There was a blinding white flash of light, and the next moment – *Bang! Crack!* A huge impact like a gigantic blow smote down upon our bodies, our heads and our hospital. I lay flat – I didn't know whether or not of my own volition.[4] Then came down piles of debris,[5] slamming onto my back.

The hospital has been hit, I thought. I grew dizzy, and my ears sang.

Some minutes or so must have passed before I staggered to my feet and looked around. The air was heavy with yellow smoke; white flakes of powder drifted about; it was strangely dark.

Thank God, I thought – I'm not hurt! But what about the patients?

As it became brighter, little by little our situation grew clearer. Miss Murai, who had been assisting me with the pneumo-thorax, struggled to her feet beside me. She didn't seem to have been seriously injured, though she was completely covered with white dust. 'Hey, cheer up!' I said. 'We're not hurt, thank God!'

---

[4] **volition:** wish
[5] **debris:** wreckage

I helped her to her feet. Another nurse, who was also in the consulting room, and the patient, managed to stand up. The man, his face smeared white like a clown and streaked with blood, lurched towards the door, holding his bloody head with his hands and moaning.

I said to myself over and over again: Our hospital has suffered a direct hit – We've been bombed! Because the hospital stood on a hill and had walls of red brick, it must, I thought, have attracted the attention of enemy planes. I felt deeply and personally responsible for what had happened.

The pervading[6] dingy yellow silence of the room now resounded with faint cries – 'Help!' The surface of the walls and ceiling had peeled away. What I had thought to be clouds of dust or smoke was whirling brick-dust and plaster. Neither the pneumo-thorax apparatus nor the micro-scope on my desk were anywhere to be seen. I felt as if I were dreaming.

I encouraged Miss Murai, saying: 'Come on, we haven't been hurt at all, by the grace of God. We must rescue the in-patients.' But privately I thought it must be all over with them – the second and third floors must have disintegrated, I thought.

We went to the door of the consulting room which faced the main stairway, and there were the in-patients coming down the steps crying: 'Help me, doctor! Oh, help me, sir.' The stairs and the corridor were heaped with timbers, plasters, debris from the ceiling. It made walking difficult. The patients staggered down towards us, crying: 'I'm hurt! Help me!' Strangely, none seemed to have been seriously injured, only slightly wounded, with fresh blood dripping from their faces and hands.

If the bomb had actually hit the hospital, I thought, they would have been far more badly injured.

'What's happened to the second and third floors?' I cried. But all they answered was – 'Help me! Help!'

---

[6] **pervading:** present everywhere

One of them said: 'Mr Yamaguchi has been buried under the debris. Help him.'

No one knew what had happened. A huge force had been released above our heads. What it was, nobody knew. Had it been several tons of bombs, or the suicidal destruction of a plane carrying a heavy bomb-load?

Dazed, I retreated into the consulting room, in which the only upright object on the rubbish-strewn floor was my desk. I went and sat on it and looked out of the window at the yard and the outside world. There was not a single pane of glass in the window, not even a frame – all had been completely blown away. Out in the yard dun-coloured smoke or dust cleared little by little. I saw figures running. Then, looking to the south-west, I was stunned. The sky was as dark as pitch, covered with dense clouds of smoke; under that blackness, over the earth, hung a yellow-brown fog. Gradually the veiled ground became visible, and the view beyond rooted me to the spot with horror.

All the buildings I could see were on fire; large ones and small ones and those with straw-thatched roofs. Further off along the valley, Urakami Church, the largest Catholic church in the east, was ablaze. The technical school, a large two-storeyed wooden building, was on fire, as were many houses and the distant ordnance[7] factory. Electricity poles were wrapped in flame like so many pieces of kindling. Trees on the near-by hills were smoking, as were the leaves of sweet potatoes in the fields. To say that everything burned is not enough. It seemed as if the earth itself emitted fire and smoke, flames that writhed up and erupted from underground. The sky was dark, the ground was scarlet, and in between hung clouds of yellowish smoke. Three kinds of colour – black, yellow and scarlet – loomed ominously over the people, who ran about like so many ants seeking to escape. What had happened? Urakami Hospital

---

[7] **ordnance:** military supplies

had not been bombed – I understood that much. But that ocean of fire, that sky of smoke! It seemed like the end of the world.

I said to myself: Yes, we must first of all rescue those seriously ill tubercular patients who've been buried under the ruins.

I looked southwards again, and the sight of Nagasaki city in a sea of flames as far as the eye could see made me think that such destruction could only have been caused by thousands of bombers, carpet-bombing. But not a plane was to be seen or heard, although even the leaves of potatoes and carrots at my feet were scorched and smouldering. The electricity cables must have exploded underground, I thought.

And then at last I identified the destroyer – 'That's it!' I cried, 'It was the new bomb – the one used on Hiroshima!'

Ten or twenty minutes after the smoke had cleared outside, people began coming up the hill from the town below, crying out and groaning: 'Help me, help!' Those cries and groans seemed not to be made by human voices; they sounded unearthly, weird.

About ten minutes after the explosion, a big man, half-naked, holding his head between his hands, came into the yard towards me, making sounds that seemed to be dragged from the pit of his stomach.

'Got hurt, sir,' he groaned; he shivered as if he were cold. 'I'm hurt.'

I stared at him, at the strange-looking man. Then I saw it was Mr Zenjiro Tsujimoto, a market-gardener and a friendly neighbour to me and the hospital. I wondered what had happened to the robust Zenjiro.

'What's the matter with you, Tsujimoto?' I asked him, holding him in my arms.

'In the pumpkin field over there – getting pumpkins for the patients – got hurt ... ' he said, speaking brokenly and breathing feebly.

It was all he could do to keep standing. Yet it didn't occur to me that he had been seriously injured.

'Come along now,' I said. 'You are perfectly all right, I assure you.

Where's your shirt? Lie down and rest somewhere where it's cool. I'll be with you in a moment.'

His head and face were whitish; his hair was singed. It was because his eyelashes had been scorched away that he seemed so bleary-eyed. He was half-naked because his shirt had been burned from his back in a single flash. But I wasn't aware of such facts. I gazed at him as he reeled about with his head between his hands. What a change had come over this man who was stronger than a horse, whom I had last seen earlier that morning. It's as if he's been struck by lightning, I thought.

After Mr Tsujimoto came staggering up to me, another person who looked just like him wandered into the yard. Who he was and where he had come from I had no idea. 'Help me,' he said, groaning, half-naked, holding his head between his hands. He sat down, exhausted. 'Water ... Water ... ' he whispered.

'What's the trouble? What's wrong with you? What's become of your shirt?' I demanded.

'Hot – *hot* ... Water ... I'm burning.' They were the only words that were articulate.[8]

As time passed, more and more people in a similar plight came up to the hospital – ten minutes, twenty minutes, an hour after the explosion. All were of the same appearance, sounded the same. 'I'm hurt, *hurt!* I'm burning! Water!' They all moaned the same lament. I shuddered. Half-naked or stark naked, they walked with strange, slow steps, groaning from deep inside themselves as if they had travelled from the depths of hell. They looked whitish; their faces were like masks. I felt as if I were dreaming, watching pallid ghosts processing slowly in one direction – as in a dream I had once dreamt in my childhood.

These ghosts came on foot uphill towards the hospital, from the direction of the burning city and from the more easterly ordnance factory. Worker or student, girl or man, they all walked slowly and had the same

---

[8] **articulate:** clearly expressed

mask-like face. Each one groaned and cried for help. Their cries grew in strength as the people increased in number, sounding like something from the Buddhist scriptures, re-echoing everywhere, as if the earth itself were in pain.

One victim who managed to reach the hospital yard asked me, 'Is this a hospital?' before suddenly collapsing on the ground. There were those who lay stiffly where they fell beside the roadside in front of the hospital; others lay in the sweet-potato fields. Many went down to the steep valley below the hospital where a stream ran down between the hill of Motohara and the next hill. 'Water, water,' they cried. They went instinctively down to the banks of the stream, because their bodies had been scorched and their throats were parched and inflamed; they were thirsty. I didn't realise then that these were the symptoms of 'flash-burn'.

The sun shone dim and reddish through the south-westerly veil of black smoke over the city. It seemed a long time since the explosion. I thought it must now be evening, but only three hours had passed. It was just two o'clock and broad daylight. I had completely lost any sense of time. And I was not alone – it was a timeless day for everyone. It seemed as if years had passed, maybe because so many houses continued to burn and because so many badly injured people appeared one after another before my eyes. On the other hand, it felt as if only a moment had passed, because all around us people and houses and fields seemed unbelievably changed.

Not every part of the hospital was beset with fire. Brother Iwanaga and I went in and out of the building many times, for I still had to make sure that all the patients and staff were safe and to check for any dead or wounded. We couldn't imagine how everything had looked before the explosion – rooms, corridors, furniture and the rest. The ceilings had all been stripped of their planks and plaster, the walls of their panelling. Desks, cupboards, bookcases, instrument boxes, medicine chests had all been overturned. Whatever had escaped the onslaught had been emptied – drawers were open and their contents lost. I never found out what happened to the contents of my desk. A gigantic wind had struck the hospital, shattered the windows, torn through every room, swept along the corridors and ravaged everything inside the hospital with a force beyond human comprehension.

It is the mark of the devil, I thought – of the devil's claw …

In the afternoon a change was noticeable in the appearance of the injured people who came up to the hospital. The crowd of ghosts which had looked whitish in the morning were now burned black. Their hair was burnt; their skin, which was charred and blackened, blistered and peeled. Such were those who now came toiling up to the hospital yard and fell there weakly.

'Are you a doctor? Please, if you wouldn't mind, could you examine me?' So said a young man.

'Cheer up!' I said. It was all I could say.

He died in the night. He must have been one of the many medical students who were injured down at the medical college. His politeness and then his poor blackened body lying dead on the concrete are things I shall never forget.

Neither shall I ever forget the countenance of a father who came stumbling up to me, carrying his baby in his arms. The father begged me to try to do something for his baby. I examined the child. The wall of its stomach had been sliced open and part of its intestines protruded. The baby's face was purple. No pulse could be felt.

I said, 'It's hopeless.'

The father, laying his baby on the grass in the yard, sat down exhausted and said: 'Would you do what you can?'

I shook my head. There was nothing that I could do. I had neither medical instruments nor medicine. He wouldn't leave the child.

The brick wall around the hospital was in ruins, blown down by the blast. The wall, hundreds of metres long, had like everything else been crushed by a devilish force. A child who had been playing near the wall lay beneath it on the road, his skull broken like a pomegranate.

Gradually the severity of cases increased: a person whose body had been riven by pieces of glass or splinters blown by the colossal force of the blast; a person who had been battered by heavy objects falling upon him; a person who had been blown off his feet and thrown against something hard – people with such serious injuries appeared one after the other. None of them, however, knew how they had come to be so badly injured. They all trembled with fear and pain, each thinking that the bomb had fallen only on them.

The southern sky was still dark. After the strange clouds caused by the explosion had thinned, smoke from the burning city obscured the sky. Through it the sun shone redly now and again. Sometimes the sound of aeroplane engines could be heard overhead – not Japanese planes, but those of the enemy. Because of the smoke we couldn't see them. The droning sound of the enemy's low-altitude flights was repeated several times, and every time the sound was heard the injured trembled, fled and hid, fearing that another bomb would be dropped or that machine-gun fire would sweep through them. Whenever the sound of the engines was heard we stopped whatever we were doing and hid, thinking the enemy were about to attack again with even greater ferocity.

I thought it unlikely, however, that they would drop any more bombs on us after the new bomb. Possibly the planes were flying over on reconnaissance,[9] checking on the damage the bomb had done. But the injured who ran about below, seeking to survive any further attack, and the people caring for the injured could not reason as objectively as I. The throb of engines made all of us tremble and cower, and the hateful sound

---

[9] **on reconnaissance:** seeing what has happened

continued off and on, endlessly, as it would even through the night, droning above the city where the black smoke hung in heavy clouds.

'Isn't all this destruction enough?' I cried, and bit my lip in mortification.

Activities

Close study (memoir: non-fiction recount text)

1 The 9 August was an exceptional day for Nagasaki and for world history. The doctor begins his record by stressing the ordinariness of daily routine up to 11 am on that fatal day. What were some of the routine things he mentions? What rumour did he hear from the engineer?

2 What was ironic about the doctor's observation of the air-raid and its alarm? What did he notice as the bomb went off? What did he observe in the aftermath? What did he see as he looked out over Nagasaki?

3 Survivors streamed up to the hospital for help. What was strange about them? What does the doctor mean by 'the devil's claw'? Which were the most tragic of the casualties he saw? What were his final thoughts about the destruction caused by the bomb?

Language study

4 Only a few people lived to tell of their experience of atomic attack. Akizuki uses comparisons to help us understand. Find some of these and comment on their effect.

Writing

5 (Extracts on pages 143–162) Taking evidence from the two passages and, if possible, the website listed on page 142, write a debate speech arguing for or against the use of nuclear weapons in war.

6 (Extracts on pages 143–162) Write a poem contrasting life in either city before, and after, the bombing.

Vietnam War (1959–1975)

After independence in 1954, French Indo-China in South East Asia was divided into two countries, North Vietnam (communist) and South Vietnam (pro-western). Communist guerrillas (Viet Cong) fought to take over the South. After 1964, the USA was drawn into the conflict, holding back the 1972 invasion by the North through air power, but losing steadily (at a final cost of 47,000 men) on the ground. A second Northern invasion of 1975 culminated in the fall of the Southern capital, Saigon, after American forces had withdrawn two years earlier.

Resources for pages 164–173

Websites www.illyria.com/tobhp.html
   www.pbs.org/wgbh/amex/vietnam/index/html

Step Lightly

Tim O'Brien from *If I Die in a Combat Zone: Box Me Up and Ship Me Home* (1973)

Tim O'Brien (b.1946) served in Vietnam as an infantryman and remains haunted by the experience. Born in Minnesota, he graduated in political science at Maccalester College in 1968. He opposed the Vietnam War, thinking it 'wrongly conceived and poorly justified'. But he did not resist the draft, not wanting to upset his parents who had both served in the Second World War. He was posted to the infantry (1969–70) in the dangerous Quang Ngai province. He hated but endured his tour of duty, and was awarded the Purple Heart medal.

On his return, he studied at Harvard University and then became a reporter on The Washington Post. *As a soldier he had sent word sketches of his Vietnam experiences to Minnesota newspapers. Now he developed them into a book,* If I Die in a Combat Zone: Box Me Up and Ship Me Home *(1973), whose title comes from an army marching song. The novel* Going After Cacciato *(1978) followed: it has been called 'the book about Vietnam'. Another set of powerful sketches,* The Things They Carried, *appeared in 1990.*

Vietnam produced a new kind of warfare. Unable to defeat the armed power of the USA in face-to-face combat, the North Vietnamese became a phantom enemy, engaging in a cunning guerrilla campaign which lured American forces into a landscape strewn with booby-trap mines. The Vietcong, the Northern soldiers, hid in tunnels or melted into the population of villages. In 'Step Lightly' O'Brien describes the nightmare of this war that cannot be won but which endlessly maims and kills individual soldiers.

The Bouncing Betty is feared most. It is a common mine. It leaps out of its nest in the earth, and when it hits its apex,[1] it explodes, reliable and deadly. If a fellow is lucky and if the mine is in an old emplacement, having been exposed to the rains, he may notice its three prongs jutting out of the clay. The prongs serve as the Bouncing Betty's firing device. Step on them, and the unlucky soldier will hear a muffled explosion; that's the initial charge sending the mine on its one-yard leap into the sky. The fellow takes another step and begins the next and his backside is bleeding and he's dead. We call it 'ol' step and a half'.

More destructive than the Bouncing Betty are the booby-trapped mortar and artillery rounds.[2] They hang from trees. They nestle in shrubbery. They lie under the sand. They wait beneath the mud floors of huts. They haunted us. Chip, my black buddy from Orlando, strayed into a hedgerow and triggered a rigged 105 artillery round. He died in such a way that, for once, you could never know his colour. He was wrapped in a plastic body bag, we popped smoke, and a helicopter took him away, my friend. And there was Shorty, a volatile fellow[3] so convinced that the mines would take him that he spent a month AWOL.[4] In July he came back to the field, joking but still unsure of it all. One day, when it was very hot, he sat on a booby-trapped 155 round.

When you are ordered to march through areas such as Pinkville – GI[5] slang for Song My, parent village of My Lai – the Batangan Peninsula or the Athletic Field, appropriately named for its flat acreage of grass and rice paddy, when you step about these pieces of ground, you do some thinking. You hallucinate. You look ahead a few paces and wonder what your legs will resemble if there is more to the earth in that spot than silicates and nitrogen. Will the pain be unbearable? Will you scream or fall

---

[1] **apex:** highest point
[2] **rounds:** shells
[3] **a volatile fellow:** a man with moods that change quickly
[4] **AWOL:** absent without leave
[5] **GI:** US infantryman

silent? Will you be afraid to look at your own body, afraid of the sight of your own red flesh and white bone? You wonder if the medic remembered his morphine. You wonder if your friends will weep.

It is not easy to fight this sort of self-defeating fear, but you try. You decide to be ultracareful – the hard-nosed, realistic approach. You try to second-guess the mine. Should you put your foot to that flat rock or the clump of weed to its rear? Paddy dike or water? You wish you were Tarzan, able to swing with the vines. You try to trace the footprints of the man to your front. You give it up when he curses you for following too closely; better one man dead than two.

The moment-to-moment, step-by-step decision-making preys on your mind. The effect sometimes is paralysis. You are slow to rise from rest breaks. You walk like a wooden man, like a toy soldier out of Victor Herbert's *Babes in Toyland*. Contrary to military and parental training, you walk with your eyes pinned to the dirt,[6] spine arched, and you are shivering, shoulders hunched. If you are not overwhelmed by complete catatonia,[7] you may react as Philip did on the day he was told to police up one of his friends, victim of an antipersonnel mine. Afterwards as dusk fell, Philip was swinging his entrenching tool like a madman, sweating and crying and hollering. He dug a foxhole four feet into the clay. He sat in it and sobbed. Everyone – all his friends and all the officers – was very quiet, and not a person said anything. No one comforted him until it was very dark. Then, to stop the noise, one man at a time would talk to him, each of us saying he understood and that tomorrow it would all be over. The captain said he would get Philip to the rear, find him a job driving a truck or painting fences.

Once in a great while we would talk seriously about the mines. 'It's more than the fear of death that chews on your mind,' one soldier, nineteen years old, eight months in the field, said. 'It's an absurd combination of certainty and uncertainty: the certainty that you're walking in mine

---

[6] **dirt:** soil

[7] **catatonia:** immobility

fields, walking past the things day after day; the uncertainty of your every movement, of which way to shift your weight, of where to sit down.

'There are so many ways the VC[8] can do it. So many configurations, so many types of camouflage to hide them. I'm ready to go home.'

The kid is right:

The M-14 antipersonnel mine, nicknamed the 'toe popper'. It will take a hunk out of your foot. Smitty lost a set of toes. Another man who is now just a blur of grey eyes and brown hair – he was with us for only a week – lost his left heel.

The booby-trapped grenade. Picture a bushy scrub along your path of march. Picture a tin can secured to the shrub, open and directed toward the trail. Inside the can is a hand grenade, safety pin removed, so that only the can's metal circumference prevents the 'spoon', or firing handle, from jumping off the grenade and detonating it. Finally, a trip wire is attached to the grenade, extending across the pathway, perhaps six inches above the dirt. Hence, when your delicate size-eight foot caresses that wire, the grenade is yanked from its container, releasing the spoon and creating problems for you and your future.

The Soviet TMB and the Chinese antitank mines. Although designed to detonate under the pressure of heavy vehicles, the antitank mine is known to have shredded more than one soldier.

The directional-fragmentation mine. The concave-faced directional mine contains from 450 to 800 steel fragments embedded in a matrix[9] and backed by an explosive charge – TNT or petnam. The mine is aimed at your anticipated route of march. Your counterpart in uniform, a gentle young man, crouches in the jungle, just off the trail. When you are in range, he squeezes his electronic firing device. The effects of the mine are similar to those of a twelve-gauge shotgun fired at close range. United

---

[8] **VC:** Viet Cong (North Vietnam army)

[9] **matrix:** substance in which things are embedded

States Army training manuals describe this country's equivalent device, the Claymore mine: 'It will allow for wider distribution and use, particularly in large cities. It will effect considerable savings in materials and logistics.' In addition, they call the mine cold-blooded.

The corrosive-action-car-killer. The CACK is nothing more than a grenade, its safety pin extracted and spoon held in place by a rubber band. It is deposited in your gas[10] tank. Little boys and men of the cloth[11] are particularly able to manoeuvre next to an unattended vehicle and do the deed – beneath a universal cloak of innocence. The corrosive action of the gasoline eats away the rubber band, releasing the spoon, blowing you up in a week or less. Although it is rarely encountered by the footborne infantryman, the device gives the rear-echelon mine finder (REMF) something to ponder as he delivers the general's laundry.

In the three days that I spent writing this, mines and men came together three more times. Seven more legs were out on the red clay; also, another arm.

The immediacy of the last explosion – three legs, ten minutes ago – made me ready to burn the midsection of this report, the flippant itemisation of these killer devices. Hearing over the radio what I just did, only enough for a flashing memory of what it is all about, makes the *Catch-22*[12] jokes into a cemetery of half-truths. ▶ 'Orphan 22, this is … this is Yankee 22 … mine, mine. Two guys … legs are off … I say again, legs off … request urgent dust-off,[13] grid 711888 … give me ETA[14] … get that damn bird.'[13] Tactical Operations Centre: 'You're coming in distorted … Yankee 22? Say again … speak slowly … understand you need dust-off helicopter?' Pause. 'This is Yankee 22 … for Chri … ake … need chopper[13] … two men, legs are … ' ◀

---

[10] **gas:** petrol
[11] **men of the cloth:** priests
[12] **Catch-22:** famous anti-war novel
[13] **dust-off/bird/chopper:** helicopter
[14] **ETA:** estimated time of arrival

But only to say another truth will I let the half-truths stand. The catalogue of mines will be retained, because that is how we talked about them, with a funny laugh, flippantly, with a chuckle. It is funny. It's absurd.

Patent absurdity. The troops are going home, and the war has not been won, even with a quarter of the United States Army fighting it. We slay one of them, hit a mine, kill another, hit another mine. It is funny. We walk through the mines, trying to catch the Viet Cong Forty-eighth Battalion like an unexperienced hunter after a hummingbird. But he finds us far more often that we do him. He is hidden among the mass of civilians or in tunnels or in jungles. So we walk to find him, stalking the mythical, phantomlike Forty-eighth Battalion from here to there to here to there. And each piece of ground left behind is his from the moment we are gone on our next hunt. It is not a war fought for territory, not for pieces of land that will be won and held. It is not a war fought to win the hearts of the Vietnamese nationals, not in the wake of contempt drawn on our faces and on theirs, not in the wake of a burning village, a trampled rice paddy, a battered detainee. If land is not won and if hearts are at best left indifferent; if the only obvious criterion of military success is body count and if the enemy absorbs losses as he has, still able to lure us amid his crop of mines; if soldiers are being withdrawn, with more to go later and later and later; if legs make me more of a man, and they surely do, my soul and character and capacity to love notwithstanding; if any of this is truth, a soldier can only do his walking laughing along the way and taking a funny, crooked step.

After the war, he can begin to be bitter. Those who point at and degrade his bitterness, those who declare it's all a part of war and that this is a job which must be done – to those patriots I will recommend a post-war vacation to this land, where they can swim in the sea, lounge under a fine sun, stroll in the quaint countryside, wife and son in hand. Certainly, there will be a mine or two still in the earth. Alpha Company did not detonate all of them.

Activities

Close study (non-fiction memoir: recount text)

1 O'Brien gives us a 'catalogue' of mines used by the Viet Cong enemy. Describe the particular horrors of each.

2 Some of O'Brien's friends were victims of mines. What happened to each one?

3 He tells us about the intense stress of advancing across mine-infested country. What is his vision of what might happen? How might a soldier try to escape danger? Why does the pursuit of the enemy seem futile? Why is the war unwinnable?

4 O'Brien takes a sardonic view of events and jokes grimly about the mines and casualties. Yet he is bitter about the soldiers' suffering and about people at home who belittle their efforts. What fate does he design for these complacent civilians after the war?

Language study

5 O'Brien half jokes about the mines and the dangers they present. He writes 'flippantly, with a chuckle. It is funny. It's absurd'. Find some phrases and sentences that express this black comedy.

6 The horrors are blunt and savage. Find some words and phrases which describe these.

7 Look at the radio exchange (from '"Orphan 22 ... "' to '"legs are ... "' (page 169)). Why is the language so dramatic and effective here?

8 Which words make the bitterness of the final paragraph so deadly?

Writing

9 Read 'Ambush', another of O'Brien's Vietnam war sketches. Compare the content and style with those of 'Step Lightly'. Which is more impressive as a statement of the horrors of war?

Ambush

When she was nine, my daughter Kathleen asked if I had ever killed anyone. She knew about the war; she knew I'd been a soldier. 'You keep writing these war stories,' she said, 'so I guess you must've killed somebody.' It was a difficult moment, but I did what seemed right, which was to say, 'Of course not,' and then to take her onto my lap and hold her for a while. Someday, I hope, she'll ask again. But here I want to pretend she's a grown-up. I want to tell her exactly what happened, or what I remember happening, and then I want to say to her that as a little girl she was absolutely right. This is why I keep writing war stories:

He was a short, slender young man of about twenty. I was afraid of him – afraid of something – and as he passed me on the trail I threw a grenade that exploded at his feet and killed him.

Or to go back:

Shortly after midnight we moved into the ambush site outside My Khe. The whole platoon was there, spread out in the dense brush along the trail, and for five hours nothing at all happened. We were working in two-man teams – one man on guard while the other slept, switching off every two hours – and I remember it was still dark when Kiowa shook me awake for the final watch. The night was foggy and hot. For the first few moments I felt lost, not sure about directions, groping for my helmet and weapon. I reached out and found three grenades and lined them up in front of me; the pins had already been straightened for quick throwing. And then for maybe half an hour I kneeled there and waited. Very gradually, in tiny slivers, dawn began to break through the fog, and from my position in the brush I could see ten or fifteen metres up the trail. The mosquitoes were fierce. I remember slapping at them, wondering if I should wake up Kiowa and ask for some repellent, then thinking it was a bad idea, then looking up and seeing the young man come out of the fog. He wore black clothing and rubber sandals and a grey ammunition belt. His shoulders were slightly stooped, his head cocked to the side as if listening for something. He seemed at ease. He carried his weapon in one hand, muzzle down, moving without any hurry up the centre of the trail. There was no sound at all – none that I can remember. In a way, it seemed, he was part of the morning fog, or my own imagination, but there was also the reality of what was happening in my stomach. I had already pulled the pin on a grenade. I had come up to a crouch. It was entirely automatic. I did not hate the young man; I did not see him as the enemy; I did not ponder issues of morality or politics or military duty. I crouched and kept my head low. I tried to swallow whatever was rising from my stomach, which tasted like lemonade, something fruity and sour. I was terrified. There were no thoughts about killing. The grenade was to make him go away – just evaporate – and I leaned back and felt my mind go empty and then felt it fill up again. I had already thrown the grenade before telling myself to throw it. The brush was thick and I had to lob it high, not aiming, and I remember the grenade seeming to freeze above me for an instant, as if a camera had clicked, and I remember ducking down and holding my breath and seeing little wisps of fog rise from the earth. The grenade bounced once and rolled across the trail. I did not hear it, but there must've been a sound, because the young man dropped his weapon and began to run, just two or three quick steps, then he hesitated, swivelling to his right, and he glanced down at the grenade and tried to cover his head but never did. It occurred to me then that he was about to die. I wanted to warn him. The grenade made a popping noise – not soft but not loud either – not what I'd expected – and there was a puff of dust and smoke – a small white puff – and the young man seemed to jerk upward as if pulled by invisible wires. He fell on his back. His rubber sandals had been blown off. There was no wind. He lay at the centre of the trail, his right leg bent beneath him, his right eye shut, his left eye a huge star-shaped hole.

It was not a matter of live or die. There was no real peril. Almost certainly the young man would have passed by. And it will always be that way.

Later, I remember, Lieutenant Cross and Kiowa tried to tell me that the man would've died anyway. They told me that it was a good kill, that I was a soldier and this was a war, that I should shape up and stop staring and ask myself what the dead man would've done if things were reversed.

None of it mattered. The words seemed far too complicated, too abstract, and all I could do was gape at the fact of the young man's body.

Even now I haven't finished sorting it out. Sometimes I forgive myself, other times I don't. In the ordinary hours of life I try not to dwell on it, but now and then, when I'm reading a newspaper or just sitting alone in a room, I'll look up and see the young man coming out of the morning fog. I'll watch him walk toward me, his shoulders slightly stooped, his head cocked to the side, and he'll pass within a few yards of me and suddenly smile at some secret thought and then continue up the trail to where it bends back into the fog.

Reading

9 Other O'Brien episodes and sketches of Vietnam that you might like to read are available in 'If I Die in a Combat Zone' and 'The Things They Carried'.

10 You might also like to read *The Vietnam War* by M.K. Hall.

General Activities

Writing tasks

1 Choose two stories, one pre- and one post-1914, that impressed you in their pictures of the horror of war. Compare what happens in each story and discuss the techniques used by each writer to express his or her ideas.

2 Choose some stories in which women are involved. Write about the ideas and language of the stories. How do they show the effect of war on women?

3 Choose two stories which are angry and bitter about war and its effects. Discuss the themes and style of each. Which is more memorable?

4 The stories clearly show the changes in the techniques of warfare in the nineteenth and twentieth centuries, in its weaponry and the ways in which it is fought. Illustrate this from a range of stories, referring closely to the texts.

5 Find two characters who are memorable in this set of stories. What are they like and how does war affect them? Refer closely to the stories.

6 Write about two stories where settings are important. How do these backgrounds contribute to the ideas expressed by the authors?

7 Think of two stories, one pre- and one post-1914, which make you feel sympathy for people caught up in war. Describe these people and their situations. How do the writers use language to create this sympathy? Which story is more impressive?

8 Some of these stories are about hostility and understanding between:
   • the generations
   • soldiers and civilians
   • fighting troops and those in authority.
   Illustrate any two of these from any two stories. Look closely at storyline, character and language.

9 Which one story that you have studied shows the misery, waste and suffering of war most forcibly? Consider the content of the story and the way in which it is written.

Spoken tasks

10 Which is the best story in *War Stories*? Form a group with others who all choose their favourites. Each person argues a case for a story, referring closely to its content and technique.

11 Give a talk to the class on a chosen story that you admire. Describe briefly what happens in the story, and comment on its characters, setting and ideas. Read some parts of the story aloud to illustrate your commentary.

12 Which war, according to this selection, produced the most powerful war stories? Each person in a group chooses a different war and argues the case.

Advanced Questions

1 This collection includes short stories and non-fiction texts. Which genre is more effective in portraying the drama and horror of war? Refer closely to several texts, looking closely at the writers' language as well as their themes and attitudes.
2 In his poem 'Strange Meeting' Wilfred Owen wrote of 'The pity of war, the pity war distilled'. Where do you find this concept most memorably displayed in *War Stories*? Consider a variety of texts, fiction and non-fiction.
3 How is women's changing experience of war reflected in this collection? Include pre-twentieth century and twentieth century writing in your answer.
4 Writing in wartime often comments on the gulf between the civilian's and the soldier's experience of war. Concentrating on two or three stories or non-fiction pieces, illustrate and discuss this theme.
5 Richard Aldington, the soldier poet, described comradeship in war as 'an undemonstrative exchange of sympathies between ordinary men racked to extremity'. How do these stories and episodes deal with the idea of comradeship? Refer closely to two or three texts.
6 War is a strange mixture of courage and futility. Write about these contrasting themes as they are revealed in this selection of stories and non-fiction writing.

Acknowledgements

The publishers gratefully acknowledge the following for permission to reproduce copyright material. Every effort has been made to trace copyright holders, but in some cases has proved impossible. The publishers would be happy to hear from any copyright holder that has not been acknowledged.

Extract from *Extract from Not So Quite ... Stepdaughters of War* by Helen Zenna Smith, published by Virago. Copyright © Helen Zenna Smith, 1988. Reprinted with permission of A.M. Heath & Co Limited, Authors' Agents.

Extract from *Their Finest Hour: Britain at War 1940* edited by Allan Mackie and Walter Graebner. Reprinted with permission of Allen & Unwin.

Extract from *Vessel of Sadness* by William Woodruff, published by J.M. Dent, 1985. Copyright © William Woodruff. Reprinted with permission of the author.

Extract from *Nagasaki 1945* by Tatsuichiro Akizuki, translated by Keuchi Nagata and edited by Gordon Honeycombe. Reprinted with permission of Peters Fraser & Dunlop Group Limited on behalf of the translator and the editor.

Extract from *If I Die in a Combat Zone: Box Me Up and Ship Me Home* by Tim O'Brien, published by Marian Boyars Publisers. Copyright © Tim O'Brien 1969. Reprinted with permission of Marion Boyars Publishers Limited.